A STRAIGHT SHOOTER IN SIDEWINDER TERRITORY

George Netfield, proprietor of Kirkville's leading saloon, was a calm, deliberate man—a man who knew what
he wanted. And what he wanted most was to root out
the rustlers that wanted to make a ghost town out of
brawling, prosperous Kirkville.

The forces he opposed were ruthless and clever—so
much so that they fooled the very ranch owner they
were robbing. Without even the help of the victim, Netfield had to find a way to unmask the marauders and
catch them red-handed in their cattle swindle. If he
failed he knew there'd be wholesale slaughter in Kirkville, and that he'd be the first to get a six-gun send-off!

CAST OF CHARACTERS

George Netfield

His cold-blooded daring made the decent people thankful he was on their side.

Sherrod Taunton Wingate

The way he fussed over, and was faithful to, his Winchester you'd think it was his wife.

The Turtle Creek Kid

Once he was faster on the draw than greased lightning, but now in his sixties, he was just the fastest man alive!

Cimarron Crewe

She knew the man she was after—but she was looking in her heart, not on her range.

Elton Colfax

As foreman of the C Bar C, he was obviously the wrong man for the job.

Kruger

He who calls the last shot, lives to laugh last.

THE FOURTH GUNMAN

by
MERLE CONSTINER

WILDSIDE PRESS

I

GEORGE NETFIELD sat at his desk in the backroom of the Blue Banner, frowning. In a few minutes, if things went wrong, if the red-haired kid panicked and went into action, he might very possibly find himself a dead man. It wasn't this that was bothering him, though. What really bothered him was that something was happening that he didn't understand.

The Blue Banner was not Kirkville's largest saloon but, in an unpretentious way, it was the town's most profitable. It was coldly and ruthlessly respectable. For minor difficulties, it had a good man in its bartender Clyde Gilday; in moments of emergency, which were few, it had Netfield, its owner.

It was one of the summer's hottest evenings. Netfield had just finished supper at the Jerome House. Now, very carefully, he lighted a crooked, oily cigar. He was a pensive man in his middle thirties, always drably dressed. Four years ago he had come from his home in Baxter Springs, Kansas, to this Montana country. He had seen lonesome prairies and badlands come wildly alive with ranches and cattle. Kirkville, when he arrived, was little more than a sod store and a barrel of whiskey. Now it was a thriving, violent, wealthy stock center.

Golden light from the lamp bathed his big horse-jaw. Smells and sounds came to him, the smells and sounds of an ovenlike night in a busy cattle town: the odor of horse urine and chaff from the stables, the bellowing and jingling from Main Street, and, closer at hand, the saloon odors of cowboy hair oil and bready, ancient beer. Netfield was waiting for Clyde Gilday, and he waited patiently.

At eight o'clock, Clyde came through the door from the front room, letting in behind him a garble of voices from the evening trade, cutting them off as he closed the door. He was a square-built, rocky man, pale and gray-haired,

5

blunt-tongued and bitter. He liked but one man in the world, Netfield. Netfield had picked him up, bereft of wife, destitute, and had employed him. Now they were as close as brothers. Unlike brothers, they never quarreled.

"Your nightman out front?" asked Netfield.

Clyde nodded. Red veins glowed on his lumpy nose. He was heading for supper and had just downed his appetizer, a half tumbler of rye.

"Send out to the restaurant for a plate of food and eat it on the bar," said Netfield. "All right? We'll want you on duty tonight."

"If you say so," said Clyde. "Of course. But why?"

"We're going to be without help. I'm firing your new man."

"Well," said Clyde, and set his teeth. "What's he done?"

"Nothing."

"I see," said Clyde. He said it softly and harshly. "This don't sound like you, George, but a man can never tell. Now it comes out, now you've got to show me you're the boss. I hire a man, just one man, because he's a friend, and you fire him. G. H. Netfield owns this place, and does the hiring and firing, and nobody else, and I'd better get it through my thick head. Is that it? Maybe you'll fire me next."

"Not likely," said Netfield gently. That old unstable, beaten look was back in Clyde's eye. The look that Netfield had tried so patiently to erase. "You say this Spunky Martin is a friend of yours. What do you know about him?"

"I didn't mean friend. I meant friend of a friend. He had a word-of-mouth recommendation from a fellow I know down in Wyoming. He come to me hungry and helpless, just like I come to you, and we needed another man, and took him on. What was wrong with that?"

"I'll tell you what was wrong with it. Spunky Martin isn't Clyde Gilday. Bring him in."

Clyde left the room and returned with the Banner's new nightman.

He was about twenty-five, thin and bony and hunched. His hair was copper red and his golden-brown skin was splattered with freckles. His cheekbones were like walnuts, and behind them, tiny eyes twinkled in deep sockets. To about everyone but Netfield, he seemed merry and frolicsome. He was already known around town for his quick laugh and flapping quillwork vest. In three days, he had become a great favorite with Blue Banner customers. Now he rocked on his heels, slapped his palms, and waited, grinning pleasantly.

"I think I'm going to fire you," said Netfield. "But first, answer me this. Are you on the dodge?"

Spunky sobered. "No. And that's the God's truth."

"Then you're fired," said Netfield.

Smiling a miserable, infectious smile, Spunky said, "I don't understand you, Mr. Netfield. I try to do right. What's wrong?"

"Well, to start with, I don't like you," Netfield said calmly. "But that's beside the point. Before you go, want to make ten easy dollars?"

Greed came into Spunky's eyes, and caution.

"I'll pay you ten dollars to take off that vest," said Netfield.

Spunky's hands splayed, and he stepped backward.

Now Clyde moved, and with the swiftness of a cat. Standing slightly to the rear of the red-haired kid, he grabbed his wrist in a clutch of steel, wrenched it around and up, and locked it between his shoulderblades. Spunky, his eyes glowing malevolently, made no effort to free himself or to defend himself. Gilday, with his free hand, brushed back the flaps of the quillwork vest.

Below Spunky's armpit, snuggled in a homemade holster, was a footlong .44-40, an old army revolver. It had had, somewhere along the line, a change of buttplates. Its new buttplates were of blackish stag, and bore three carefully filed notches, glinting in the kerosene lamplight.

"Turn him loose, Clyde," said Netfield. "He won't bother you."

Clyde said angrily, "He's carrying enough powder to blast ten foot of caprock."

"He certainly is," said Netfield. "But he's a professional, and it's not going to be wasted on us. He says he's not on the dodge, and I believe him, so he just carries it for business purposes. He's using us, using the Blue Banner for some reason. We don't want him behind our bar."

To Spunky, Netfield said, "All right. Get out."

"I got this gun," said Spunky glibly, "and I been living from pillar to post and don't have no place to keep it, so I carry it. What's wrong with a young feller owning a gun?"

"Get out," said Netfield.

"If you say so," said Spunky. "But I want you to remember one thing."

"What's that?" asked Clyde.

"I like you gentlemen, and I don't hold this agin you."

"Move along," said Netfield.

In the alley doorway, just before he vanished into the night, Spunky said, "No harm done. I don't bear you no grudge. I'll forget it if you forget it. I like you."

When he had gone, Clyde said, "He likes us. He said so twice. He looked meaner'n a blood-crazed Comanche when he said it, but he said it."

Netfield was thinking of other things. After a moment, he said, "What's going on? He's strictly a businessman. What's he doing here in Kirkville?"

"He's just a drifter," said Clyde. "We're shut of him. Forget him."

"I think I'll take a little walk," said Netfield.

He passed through the backdoor into the alley and turned onto Main Street, moving with slow dignity, a slim, almost shabby man, stiffly erect. People spoke to him, and he responded gently and gravely. In the corner of his mouth he clenched the dead stub of his Cuban cigar.

Nightdust hung above the blazing lights of Main Street like a lavender veil beneath an indigo sky. Down the center of Main Street ran the railroad track, dividing the town, north and south. In front of the Jerome House, four timber steps led down to the rutted road. He descended the steps, crossed the tracks, and came into the shadows of the south side of the street. Lights here were few and weak.

Continuing south, he passed through an area of weeds and shanties and reached a cross street. The houses here were unpainted, slate gray in the starless night. This was South Congress Street, better known as Piano Street. It was a confederation of Kirkville's parlor-houses. In the dictionary they called them brothels; in Denver they called them sporting establishments; but in Montana they called them parlor-houses.

He turned in at the second house in the row, ascended to the narrow porch and knocked. Behind him, like nets from the porchposts, dead honeysuckle vines obscured him from the street. The door opened, and a perfumed young woman smiled at him, then blinked.

"Why, Mr. Netfield," she said graciously. "I surely didn't expect to see *you* here."

"I didn't expect to ever be here," said Netfield politely. "Is Miss Ernestine in?"

She led him down a hall, loud with nearby music. At the end of the hall, she said, "In there," and left him.

He stepped into a small dirty kitchen. An elderly fat woman in black tafetta sat in a rockingchair, a flatiron between her bulbous knees and a hammer in her hand, cracking and eating walnuts. She had waxen, predatory eyes; at the sight of Netfield, however, they gleamed with warmth and friendship.

He had done this woman a favor once. It had been a slight favor, but he had done it earnestly, without condescension, and she had never forgotten it. He prized her friendship.

"Sit down," she said. "Have a ham sandwich and a glass of beer."

He shook his head.

They gazed at each other quietly.

After a moment, he said, "Miss Ernestine, I don't like to ask this question, but have there been any strangers, any special strangers, along Piano Street lately?"

She spit out a piece of shell. "Now why would you ask that?"

He told her about Spunky Martin.

"Yes," she said at length. "Four of them, up and down the street, coming and going. Coming separately, then chumming up, then leaving separately. Four very tough boys indeed, and your Spunky Martin is one of them."

"Four?" said Netfield. "Four? Who are the others, and where do they hang out?"

"One called Buttermilk Johnson, works at the Gem Livery-stable. Then there's Buck Smith, who works for Colonel Crewe in the wine room of the Antlers. The fourth one goes by the tag of Kruger. Doesn't work anywhere. Just seems to wander around. He's far and away the worst of the lot. I don't know where he stays. If I find out, I'll send you word."

"Thanks," said Netfield, frowning.

Amused at his concentration, she said, "Montana is getting to be as bad as Baxter Springs, isn't it?"

Netfield grinned. They stared at each other in silent communication.

That was one thing Netfield had in common with Miss Ernestine. She knew his hometown. She was one of the few people in Kirkville who knew of Baxter Springs at its peak. It had been the first of the wild, booming railheads —before Abilene, Ellsworth, before Dodge City. This was a memory fifteen years ago and a thousand miles away, but Miss Ernestine knew. Baxter Springs, in its brief day, had made ferocious history. Gunfighter and gunman, lawman and bandit—most of the great had visited it.

"Are you in trouble?" asked Miss Ernestine.

"I don't think so, no," said Netfield. He walked to the door. "But I have a feeling Kirkville is."

Main Street was already settling for the night when Netfield returned. He climbed the timber steps before the Jerome House, from road level to sidewalk level, and came to a stop before the hotel entranceway. To his left and right, up and down the porticoed boardwalk, merchants were closing, taking in their sidewalk displays of buggy whips and ax handles in headless vinegar barrels, pyramids of tinware, unhooking the denim workclothes suspended with hams and bacon slabs from the overhead portico beams. Saloons, gambling halls, and restaurants, now taking over, blazed with light.

Worried, Netfield made a double decision. First, he had better send a relief man around to the Blue Banner to take a little of the load off of Clyde. Then, of course, the intelligent and proper step was to inform Colonel Crewe. The Colonel was Kirkville's emperor. He owned not only the Antlers, but also the mammoth Kirkville Feeding Yards, about a third of Main Street, and a powerful backcountry ranch, the Hungry Butte C Bar C. He was a standoffish hard to know man. Netfield disliked him, and scarcely bothered to nod to him. An ailing man, he was becoming increasingly enfeebled, and this disability certainly wasn't going to help the interview.

Netfield was about to enter the Jerome House, when the nightclerk pushed through the door and stood beside him on the walk. He was a little potbellied man with a ceaselessly working mouth.

Now words issued from it. "Clyde's dead, George," he said. "They got him laid out in Andy's backroom."

Netfield moistened his lips. After a long pause, he asked softly, "What happened?"

"He was shot in the rear of the Gem Livery Stable, on that cleated ramp between the stalls and the main floor, in a gun fracas with that ex-barman of yours, Spunky Martin."

"He was alone, holding down the Banner," said Netfield. "He wouldn't have left it."

"Well, that's what he did. He locked it up, left a little card in the window, *Back Soon*, then went down to the livery-stable and drew against a faster man. Spunky told the law that you people had fired him earlier in the evening, and that Clyde wouldn't let it go at that but tagged along and pushed him into a fight. It must have happened just that way. The new stableman at the Gem, a fellow knowed as Butter-milk Johnson, was there and seen and heard the whole thing."

"Does that sound like Clyde?" asked Netfield harshly.

"If you want an honest answer, it sure as hell does," said the clerk. Uncomfortably, he added, "He was meaner'n a pocketful of thistles, and you know it as well as I do."

Netfield made no answer. Swinging about on his heel, he started up the walk.

II

SCARCELY a dozen establishments showed light as Netfield strode east on Main. Not a single human was in sight and along the boardwalk. Under the block-long portico, shadows hung in the doorways like patches of charcoal. To a stranger it might have seemed a street asleep, but Netfield knew it as a street very much awake. He passed the bank, a barbershop, a saddleshop, all dark, and came to the Antlers.

The Antlers was a large old clapboard building, two stories high, on the corner of Court. It was a combination of saloon, gambling hall, and hotel. It had pretensions at being a first-class place, and these very pretensions had converted it into a huge, boxlike honky-tonk. Cowhands, traveling theatrical troupes and itinerant sharpsters enjoyed its drink, entertain-ment and bed, but respectable stockmen knew it for what it was—dynamite—and gave it a wide berth.

Each of its three units was carefully separated from the

others. The hotel occupied the second story, and was reached by an outside staircase which ran up the clapboards along Court Street. The saloon proper was on the ground floor front; the two gambling rooms were behind the saloon and reached by the public through an alley door. Thus, as Colonel Crewe pointed out, there could be no accidental and unfortunate mixture of customers. That was the theory. The facts were something to the contrary. The Antlers was one big beehive of teeming trouble.

Netfield turned left down Court, and 'stopped at a small door under the framework of the outside staircase. This was the entrance to the Antlers wine room. A wine room was simply a ladies' room. This did not mean that its female customers were strictly ladies, nor did it mean that any free-spending male, dredged up from any gutter, was not more than welcome at its tables. Wine rooms produced about the same annual mortality as steamboat explosions. Netfield had no wine room at the Blue Banner.

Running his hand beneath his coatskirt, he slipped his Colt in its holster, twice, to ease it, and entered.

Perhaps a dozen people, men and women, all riffraff, were at small tables, drinking. Across a far corner of the room was a short bar, diagonally placed from wall to wall. Here were two smoky lamps; this was the only illumination. Standing before the bar, and leaning on it, a tall gangling man in filthy workclothes argued drunkenly with the barman. The barman was Tom Lenroot, an oxlike oldtimer whom Netfield knew well; the gangling man was a stranger to Netfield. All eyes but the eyes of these two lifted to Netfield as he entered.

Closing the door behind him, he stood an instant just within the threshold, inspecting the room with quick, cutting glances. To his left, alone at a table, was a blowzy, listless girl, about fifteen, in orange-red satin. This was Violet Archer, a part-time waitress at the Mockingbird Restaurant. At her throat, pinned to her dress, was a brooch about the size of a silver dollar. It was an oval, covered with glass; behind the glass were tiny knotted flowers fashioned from human hair.

This brooch had been Clyde Gilday's sole sentimental possession. It had belonged to his wife, and he had carried it ever since she had died. He kept it wrapped in oilskin in his vest pocket. He rarely displayed it. He was never without it.

Netfield said, "Good evening, Violet. Hot evening, isn't it? May I buy you a drink?"

"No," she said, smiling. "But thank you. Mr. Johnson is buying my drinks this evening."

"Mr. Johnson?"

She lifted an affected finger and pointed to the gangling man at the bar.

To be perfectly sure of his ground, Netfield rechecked. He said, "I believe that's the man I've seen around the Gem Livery Stable. Don't they call him Buttermilk?"

"Yes," she said.

"That's a lovely brooch," said Netfield. "Where did you get it?"

"Mr. Johnson gave it to me," she said. "It belonged to his dear old mother."

"Yes," said Netfield, and turned moodily away.

There was a man serving tables, but this man was not Buck Smith. He was an old Kirkville barfly known as Railroad. Netfield had bought him many a meal; in fact, at the moment, he was wearing a castoff pair of Netfield's shoes. At the moment, Railroad was leaning against the wall. His shirt was unbuttoned to the navel and he was swabbing his chest and armpits with his balled-up apron.

Approaching him, Netfield said quietly, "Buck Smith. Where is he? This is important."

"Don't mess with them people," said Railroad behind his apron. "Take my advice, Mr. Netfield. Steer shy of them."

"Where is he?"

"Taking the night off. Upstairs, in the hotel. Not in a regular room because he's just a nobody. He has him a pallet

in a kind of closet at the backend of the hall. He claims
he's got a stomach-ache."

"Then there's a man named Kruger," said Netfield. "He
been in here tonight?"

"I don't know any Kruger," said Railroad.

Netfield nodded his thanks, and walked briskly to the
bar.

The gangling man, in drunken rancor, was trying to argue
with the bartender on the subject of buffalo hunting. His
greasy calico shirt and crusty denims had a foul livery
stable stench about them. Netfield stepped beside him and
asked pleasantly, "Did you hold him while Spunky shot him?"

The man turned blearily, and batted his eyes. Foggily, he
said, "What the hell do you want?"

"First," said Netfield placidly, "I want to take a look at
you, alive."

His long, slender hand came out, big knuckled and sinewy.
It came out slowly, almost amiably, and up, and fastened
itself in a sudden savage vise in the flabby skin of Johnson's
upper throat, gathering in the V of lax flesh beneath his
chin as though it were a handful of chamois.

"You look about like I expected," said Netfield.

Johnson's hands flapped to his throat to relieve the tor-
ment. Netfield hit him. He hit him viciously, with unleashed,
jaw-cracking force, and Johnson spun, staggered, and went
to his knee. He fumbled at his gunbelt, and Netfield shot him.
Yawning in death, he threshed on the floor.

"Dust thou art, to dust returneth," said Netfield gravely,
and reholstered his gun.

All the room was staring, frozen.

Lenroot the bartender said roughly, "He was too drunk
to pull a trigger."

"Oh, I doubt that," said Netfield.

"You knocked him helpless, then stood back and shot him
like a baby."

"Not like a baby, like a snake."

"That was the most coldblooded thing I ever seen, Mr. Netfield."

"It was intended to be," said Netfield.

Before Lenroot could answer, Netfield said, "Listen, Tom. Clyde Gilday wasn't killed in any fight. This man Johnson simply cornered him in the stable and slaughtered him. With his pal Spunky Martin. Then, automatically, because they're naturally larcenous, they robbed his body. Does that sound like a fight? Do you hold with robbing dead bodies, Tom?"

"I hadn't heard any of this, Mr. Netfield."

"Well, you hear it now," said Netfield. He bent, took Johnson's .45 from its leather, slipped it in his waistband, and went to Violet Archer at her table.

"I'll have to take that brooch, Violet," he said. "I don't think you want it. It belonged to Clyde's wife."

Dazed, she handed it over.

Moving slowly and deliberately, walking stiffly, he left the wine room, and emerged once more into the sultry night.

Above him was the framework of the outside staircase. He moved to its foot, mounted the steps to a small landing, and passed into a dingy, empty rat-hole lobby. Beyond the desk with its open register was a narrow, uncarpeted hall.

He went down the hall to its dead end and found himself facing a brown, paint-blistered door with a china knob. Taking his Colt in his hand, he turned the knob and pushed inward, into a hot, stuffy cubbyhole.

The walls were unpapered and grimy, and there was no window. In one corner was a sheaf of brooms and mops and in another was a stack of pool cues, for downstairs the Antlers boasted the town's only billiard table. The patch of floor, scarcely four feet by eight, was almost entirely occupied by a tomato can with a candle on it, and a mildewed quilt with a man supine on it. The man was square-jawed, bristled, with tangled hair and, to Netfield's experienced eye, was a number-one hardcase. His hands were folded beneath his head, he was gazing unseeingly at the ceiling,

and there was a trimmed-down gun resting across his breast-
bone.

When he saw Netfield materialize before him, cocked
Colt in hand, he said soothingly, "Everything's all right,
everything's fine. Just hold steady, friend."

Despite himself, Netfield grinned.

Their eyes locked.

"Ain't you goin' to take away my weapon?" said the man.

"Why should I?"

"Now that scares me," said the man, and meant it. "I
knowed, and I told 'em—all along I told 'em—that Kirkville
could be a skillet of hard luck. Now I'm the first to go."

"You're not the first. Buttermilk Johnson was the first."

"Well, I never liked Buttermilk. But I sure as hell like
old Buck Smith—that's me. You must be Mr. Netfield."

"I am."

"Got it in your mind to kill me, ain't you?"

"That's right."

"I hadn't nothing to do with killing your friend Gilday,
but I don't expect you to believe it. That wasn't why they
brought me here, and I only do what they pay me for."

"Why was Gilday killed?"

"He got suspicious and followed Spunky to the stable and
caught him and some other fellers with their heads together,
fellers that wasn't even supposed to know each other."

"Who?"

"I'm afraid I ain't goin' to tell you that, Mr. Netfield." He
smiled sadly. "Boys, whatever become of old Buck Smith?
Didn't you hear? Seems like he went with some fellers up
into Montana and thought he was too big for his pants, and
got hisself destroyed. Old Buck Smith, the famous gunfighter."

Curiously, Netfield asked, "Are you famous?"

"Well, no. I won't die with that lie on my lips. I'm con-
siderably good, and tolerably decent according to my lights,
but I ain't truly famous."

"Where is Spunky Martin?"

"Back at the feeding yard. He went off halfcocked and Kruger got him out of the way."

"Who is Kruger?"

"Who knows? He claims to be Canadian but my secret guess is that he is from the Chiricahuas, and was Apache-raised. For one thing, he never wears nothing on his feet but moccasins."

"Where can I find him?"

"At C Bar C, I suppose."

"*C Bar C? Is he working for Colonel Crewe?*"

"Of course he ain't working for Colonel Crewe. But I can't tell you no more along that line. I'd like to, but I've took money there, and it wouldn't be right. Like I said, I'm decent according to my lights."

"Kruger isn't working for Crewe, but Spunky is? Is that right?"

"No. Not Spunky either."

"But you said he was working at the feeding yards."

"Man, not the Kirkville Feeding yards. At the feed yards at Faynopolis, down across the mountains."

"Down across the mountains," said Netfield, startled. "What's going on?"

Smith closed his eyes in wooden silence.

After a moment, Netfield said, "If I just walk out of here and forget you, what will you do?"

"I'll lay here and shiver awhile. Then I'll get up and make for New Mexico, where I come from and where I belong."

Netfield started for the door.

Smith asked, "Ain't you afraid I'll shoot you in the back?"

"Not you," said Netfield.

"That's right," said Smith. "I've shot them just about all other ways, top, bottom, north, east, south, west, and somersaulting, but I ain't never shot one in the back. Goodbye, Mr. Netfield, and good luck."

Halfway up Main Street, next door west of the Jerome House, separated from it by a broad alley, was Efferson's

Merchandise, its front window dark. Netfield turned down
the alley, walked about sixty feet, and came into a little
courtyard behind the store. Here he opened a door, and
stepped into the county-famous Efferson backroom. Andy
Efferson was Kirkville's leading merchant in rugs, furniture,
stoves, and general household equipment. He was also the
only undertaker in four thousand square miles.

The room was a workshop, low and dank, walled with
rough, hairy planking golden in the light of two barn
lanterns. There was a work table made of a house door on a
brace of sawhorses, and to one side a carpenter's bench with
a rack of woodworking tools. Andy Efferson sat alone on
a stool, hunched over a volume of Gibbons' *Decline and Fall
of the Roman Empire.* He was a scrawny, cup-cheeked man,
and his scholarly eyes had looked upon much grief. He was
Netfield's closest friend in Kirkville.

When he saw Netfield, he said simply, "Clyde's in the
storeroom, George. Want to see him?"

"No," said Netfield. On a corner of the table, he laid
the brooch, and Buttermilk Johnson's Colt. "Bury these with
him."

Efferson nodded. Gently, he said, "I'll fix him up a nice
clean pine coffin. Does that suit you?"

"No," said Netfield. "I want him buried in mahogany."

"I don't have any mahogany, George. Nobody hereabouts
uses mahogany coffins."

"You have mahogany bedsteads, don't you? You're a cab-
inetmaker, aren't you? Take some mahogany bedsteads and
square them and fit them. And I want him embalmed. I
don't want him buried like a drifter. I want you to use
the best mercuric chloride. I want the coffin lined with the
best black satin. Send across the street to the New York
Ladies Wear and get some of their best boltcloth."

"I'm going to bury him in a plain pine box," said Efferson
quietly. "That's what he would want, and that's what he's
going to get."

When Netfield made no answer, Efferson said, "You're not

trying to bury a friend, George. You're trying to bury a friendship. And no man can do that."

Netfield flushed, then nodded.

"And loosen up," said Efferson. "I've never seen your eyes so hard and crazy. Just what happened?"

Netfield told him.

When he had finished, there was nothing in the room but dankness, silence, and the reek of the lanterns.

Finally, Efferson said, "What's happening?"

"I don't know," said Netfield.

"Colonel Crewe should be informed," said Efferson.

"I'm going to inform him," said Netfield wolfishly. "Now."

"I like him, but you don't."

"That's right," said Netfield. "I don't."

As Netfield turned to leave, Efferson said, "Go easy, George. He's a mighty sick man."

Netfield merely flattened his lips.

III

COMING OUT into the courtyard, Netfield followed the alley northward. For three blocks he passed the darkened back-doors of business establishments, diminishing in size and importance, and came eventually to Fifth Street, shadowy and dusty in the night. North of Fifth lay Kirkville's best residential neighborhood. He turned into Fifth. Then north on Lafayette, and pulled up before a big house, bulky and showy, bluish silver in the moonglow.

This was the home of Colonel Crewe and his daughter Cimarron. An ornate two-story veranda ran across its front, with pendent, white-painted cornices of wooden rods and balls and fancy fan-shaped curlicues. Two-thirds of the way along the east side of the house, towards its rear, was a small porch and door for business visitors, for this was headquarters and nerve center for all of the extensive Crewe enterprises, including the C Bar C. Netfield went up the glazed brick walk, crossed the veranda, and knocked at the door. Through a diamond-shaped pane of raspberry-colored glass, he could see the elegant hall within.

He had never been in this house, or even on this porch, and he was mildly curious as to what it might hold for him.

Cimarron Crewe answered his knock. She was about twenty-eight, firmly and smoothly muscled, with the competent shoulders of a veteran horsewoman. The brownness of her skin, the deep yellow of her immaculate hair, the charcoal of her eyes, gave her a taut animal vitality. Her home was out at C Bar C. She was seldom in town, but Netfield knew her by sight.

Apparently, she knew him by sight also, for she said, "Good evening, Mr. Netfield. Did you have an appointment with my father?"

"No," said Netfield. "No appointment."

"He's a little tired tonight."

"So am I," said Netfield.

After an instant's hesitation, she led him down the hall, and into a pleasant sitting room.

There was a big stone fireplace, cold now, with a vase of artificial flowers on its hearth. The carpet was soft green, the woodwork bright cherry, and the furniture massive and comfortable. Indian lances, shields, and quivers were arranged in patterns on the chalky lemon walls. Colonel Crewe sat in a horsehair armchair by a claw-and-ball table. Tucked in his lap, on a Sioux blanket, were three knots of fur: a mother cat and two kittens. When you first looked at Colonel Crewe, Netfield realized, you simply got an impression of black broadcloth; on second look you saw a vain middle-aged man, sick, slot-eyed, and meaty.

He met Netfield's entry with glassy hostility.

"This is my sitting room, not my office," he said. "Come back tomorrow and use the side door."

Netfield gave them a brisk account of the evening's events. He began it with Spunky Martin and his shoulder gun, told them of the four strangers (not mentioning Miss Ernestine), told them of Buttermilk Johnson's death, and of Clyde's.

Colonel Crewe listened, unmoved. When Netfield had finished, the Colonel said, "Why bother me with all this?"

"They're here on something big," said Netfield. "I thought you'd like to know about it. Two of them, by the way, were employed by you. Buck Smith at the Antlers, and Kruger at C Bar C."

"And one by you," said Cimarron pleasantly. "This Spunky Martin."

Pompously, Colonel Crewe said, "These things are nothing, nothing at all. This is Montana. Gunfighters and their ilk are the manner of the times. They come and go. Are you alarmed?"

"Angry, mainly."

"And you came to solicit my help?"

Turning coldly to Cimarron, Netfield said, "How do I get out of here? I can't take this any longer."

She went with him to the door, and stood with him a moment on the shadowed veranda.

"This was unfair of you," she said sternly. "Trying to drag papa into your personal quarrels. Papa is very powerful, and very respectable, and very important."

"And very stupid," said Netfield amiably. He placed his hat on his long hair, touched its brim in polite farewell, and walked down the steps. He was dog-tired.

A nightlight burned in Efferson's Merchandise, on Netfield's return to town. He took the alley, passed through the court, and entered the storeroom. Andy was at his workbench, plane in hand, and on the floor about his ankles crisp buttery shavings lay in resinous curls.

Netfield said, "I won't be at the funeral tomorrow. I've got something to do, and I've got to do it fast, and that's the way Clyde would have wanted it. I'm taking a little ride out to C Bar C and I may be gone for a couple of days. If you see Sheriff Walsh, tell him I haven't forgotten him."

"See Colonel Crewe?" asked Efferson over his spectacle rims.

"Yes. Papa and daughter seem to think I'm in some sort
of personal trouble, and that I came to them asking for
help. I might add they didn't offer any."

Tactfully, Efferson changed the subject. "If you're headed
toward C Bar C, you may run into Sheriff Walsh himself.
He's been gone for a couple of days, up in the north end of
the county . . . bringing in a cattle thief, I understand."

"Cattle thief? Anybody I know?"

"I doubt it. They're after a very small farmer named
Wingate, from over in the Black Feather foothills."

"Never heard of him," said Netfield.

IV

C BAR C lay southeast of Kirkville, not far from the mountains. It was a long day's ride, but Netfield was well mounted
on his favorite bay, Beeswax. He made steady, mile-eating
time. By ten in the morning, he had cut a good hour from
the journey, by noon a second, and by mid-afternoon a third.
By four o'clock, though Beeswax was still moving effort-
lessly, she showed a touch of lather and Netfield brought
her to a halt to let her blow.

This was not basin country, nor valley country. It had
its basins and valleys, its buttes, breaks, and prairies, but it
was greater than all of these, which were but its components.
Between the rivers lay the prairies, in endless mottled patches
of lush grasslands and sere sage. There were two kinds of
water here in the flatlands: sweet water from distant mountain streams, and bitter, lethal water, alkali pools. In the
distance, hung the badlands, glowing blue, milk silver,
and burnt rose in the fire of the sun.

Netfield was scarcely a mile from the C Bar C line when
he decided to pause at Quinty's and rest his mount. The
road dipped, turned left, and he dismounted and hitched
his mare to the rack.

The building was a two-room cabin of twisted whitewashed logs, flush to the edge of the road. It had a dirt roof, growing with weeds and wild-flowers, and across its face was a long, low porch, earth-floored, with benches and broken chairs. This was Quinty's, a not too reputable road-ranch, pretending to cater to travelers, but, according to rumor, catering to the county's hinterland outlaw element. Quinty himself sat on his heels in the dirt before the door, munching and tearing at a slab of antelope liver. He was an emaciated little man, in stiff, stinking buckskin.

Netfield said amiably, "Open me a can of peaches and bring me some cold cornbread. I haven't eaten since day-break."

"There's nothing here," said Quinty. "I been sick. Move on."

"Water for my mount then," said Netfield. "Are you refusing me water for my mare?"

A man came out of the doorway, into the open, carrying two cedar buckets of sloshing water. He was a bulky, sullen man in a heavy, brown businessman's suit and dusty stockman's boots. His froglike eyes, peeping coldly from their tight lids of glossy purple skin, were cruel and without expression.

This man was well known to Netfield. His name was Webster Dunphy, and he was Colonel Crewe's general manager; his office and headquarters was at the Kirkville Feeding Yards. His record at the feed yards was not good; there had been rumors of short weight in the haying pens; and even a little stealing out of the yards, but the Colonel trusted him and nothing seemed to come of the suspicions.

When he had watered Netfield's bay, he said, "All right, Mr. Netfield. You're all fixed up. Now you can ride."

Netfield sat himself on a chair in the porch shade. He leaned his shoulders against the log wall, relaxed, and lighted a cigar.

Down the road, to the south, a buckboard materialized in a cloud of dust. Behind the buckboard, with shotguns across their pommels, rode three cowhands. Even from the distance, there was a sense of tenseness about the little cavalcade. It approached slowly, at a walk, and drew to a halt before the road-ranch.

On the front seat of the buckboard, driving, was Sheriff Walsh, shifty-eyed as usual, with a ribbon of dried tobacco juice running down his chin. Beside him was a young farmer, perhaps twenty-five years old, red-necked and straw-haired, with worried baby-blue eyes. Between them, on the floor, was a battered telescope valise.

The cowhands and the sheriff climbed to the ground, clustered about the young farmer, and lifted him from the seat to the earth. He stood for a moment, swaying; his ankles were fettered with cumbersome, rusty leg-irons.

The sheriff unlocked one side of the leg-irons, unfettering the farmer on one side, and then all of them walked him to the shade of the porch. He walked in a clumsy, hampered way, keeping his balance with difficulty.

Netfield knocked the ash from his cigar, and studied the cowhands. They were as tough and savage looking as any mortals he'd ever laid eyes on, but he'd never seen any of them before. His glance swept past them, to their mounts. Their horses carried the 7 Diamond brand.

7 Diamond was in Kirk County, but barely. It lay at the county's southernmost edge, beyond C Bar C, at the very foot of the mountains. Not much was known about it. It was supposed to be very small, but rich in good grass. It fraternized not at all, and any business relations it had with its neighbors were scant, courteous, and to the point. Kirkville, when it saw its punchers, which was seldom, marked them down as well mannered but offish. It was said the 7 Diamond men went out of the county and across the mountains to Faynopolis to do most of its trading.

As the group approached Netfield, he said lazily, "Afternoon, Sheriff, gentlemen, Especially, gentlemen. Any of you boys go under the name of Kruger?"

One of the punchers, with the quick movements and chin of a snake, said, "None of us, friend."

"Know where I might find him?" asked Netfield.

They shook their heads.

Now, seemingly to his amazement, Sheriff Walsh observed Webster Dunphy. "Why, howdy, Web. What you doing so far from town?"

"Why, howdy, Sheriff," said Dunphy.

The young farmer spoke, addressing Netfield. He was standing dust-smeared and stolid, and a ring of flies fed at a trickle of blood from his ear.

In an apologetic voice, he said, "It galls my heart to ask a favor of a man I never met before, but would you kindly take that Colt your wearin' and shoot all six of these maggots? I mean everybody in sight but you and me."

"You must be Wingate," said Netfield.

"That's right," said Sheriff Walsh. "And he stole eighty head of cows from these gentlemen here, from 7 Diamond."

"Did you?" asked Netfield affably.

"No," said Wingate. "But that ain't the point. The point is that everybody from 7 Diamond, plus the sheriff here, plus Quinty, too, probably, plus maybe you, will swear I did. I got a little farm between C Bar C and 7 Diamond. I proved up on my 160 acres and thought I was all set. I always been on good enough terms with C Bar C and 7 Diamond, and now this. This morning at dawn the sheriff and these boys come in on me with a mess of trouble. They packed my valise, accused me of rustling, put on these leg-irons, and now they're taking me to jail."

"Why the valise?" asked Netfield.

"I'm going to be a long time away from home, they say."

The snake-chinned puncher got into the conversation. "7 Diamond don't want to prosecute nobody, and don't take no pleasure in sending a young feller to jail. But eighty cows is no joke. It just wants its money. I keep telling Mr. Wingate that, and he keeps saying he ain't got no money, all he's got is them 160 acres of farm. If there's one thing 7 Diamond don't need, it's 160 acres of farm."

"Wait a minute," said Web Dunphy, and raised his

finger as though in meditation. All but Netfield turned to him expectantly.

"I believe I've got it," said Dunphy. "I could buy that farm and pay these boys off. We could handle it all right where we stand. I could draw up the papers, and we've got witnesses. I could write out my draft to Mr. Wingate, an he could stand right here and assign it to 7 Diamond."

"I didn't know you were interested in farming," said Netfield.

"I'm not," said Dunphy. "But I've always liked that neck of country. There's mighty good hunting, elk and such, not far away. I could build a little hunting camp—"

"The place has already got a hunting camp," said Wingate angrily. "If you could call a first-rate farm cabin a hunting camp."

"Well," said Sheriff Walsh in a suety voice. "You know what? Thanks to Mr. Dunphy, I think we got this thing all worked out."

Wingate turned to Netfield. "What shall I do?"

"Sign," said Netfield bleakly.

The papers were drawn up, signed and witnessed. The draft was drawn up, signed, and transferred.

"Goodbye Old Wingate Homestand," said Wingate.

"Now, young man," I've got something to say to you," said Sheriff Walsh sternly. "Kirk County don't cherish cow-thieves." He bent down and took off the leg-irons. "I'm ordering you to get out of this county, and pronto. Now here's what I want you to do. Get in that buckboard and drive it into Kirkville. In Kirkville, catch the next train to anywheres. These boys—Julian here—" He pointed to the snake-faced 7 Diamond leader. "Will ride along with you to see that you sure enough take it."

Netfield said, "And his suitcase is already packed."

"Correct," said the cowhand Julian.

"By the way, who packed it?"

"I did," said Julian. "As a little kindness. Whilst they was putting on his leg-irons."

"But how will *you* get to town, Sheriff," said Netfield, "if he takes your buckboard?"

"I'm visiting a spell with Quinty. I'll rent a horse from him."

Once more young Wingate consulted Netfield. "Well, what do you think?"

"To this, I think no," said Netfield.

He arose, left the porch and went to the buckboard where he snapped up the catches of the valise. Gently, he emptied its contents upon the earth. It contained a flatiron, a few pieces of broken crockery, and a couple of burlap potato sacks.

"And there," said Netfield, "are the 'necessities' they packed for you. They just threw in anything they put their hands on."

"But why?" said Wingate. "Why would they even bother to—?"

"I hate to tell you," said Netfield. "And of course no one will ever know for sure, but let's put it this way. Let's say I hadn't entered the picture at all. Let's say you'd just come here to Quinty's road ranch, with your leg-irons and suitcase. Just by luck, of course—you've heard how surprised everyone was at meeting here—Mr. Dunphy would be on hand and would buy you out of your trouble."

"Hold on there," put in Sheriff Walsh.

Netfield ignored him. He continued. "All right. Then they'd put you in the buckboard and tell you to drive into town. Maybe on the way in, someone—certainly not Julian and his friends, would shoot you. The suitcase had served its purpose, and they'd get rid of it. Its purpose was simply to keep you quiet all along. So there you are. Found dead in a buckboard. Causing nobody any trouble in the future."

Pale with rage, Sheriff Walsh said, "You're talking mighty dangerous talk, Mr. Netfield."

In a soft voice, Wingate said, "So your name is Netfield. Thank you, Mr. Netfield. What do I do now?"

"I need a new barman. Can you tend bar?"

"I can sure as hell learn."

Netfield said, "Then borrow that buckboard, as so kindly offered you, and hit for Kirkville. Look up Andy Efferson and ask him for the spare key to the Banner. You can sleep in the backroom. Tell Efferson to advance you forty dollars for your personal expenses. Tell him to give you a completely new outfit of clothes and a good six-shooter."

"I'll take it all but the six-shooter," said young Wingate. "I purely can't handle a six-shooter."

"Where did you come from, boy?" asked Dunphy.

"A little iron mining town in the heart of the Tennessee hills, called Chickasaw Furnace."

"And they didn't have six-shooters?"

"Oh, they had them, and carried them, but they didn't much favor them."

Chuckling, Sheriff Walsh asked, "What did they favor? Bows and arrows?"

"Well," said Wingate in a shy, delicate voice. "They favored dynamiting one another's cabins, and burning in the dark of the moon, and throwing strychnine in one another's springhouses, and bushwhacking from a good safe distance with a nice, true rifle. Everybody in Chicksaw Furnace loves rifles. I could never really get the hang of one of those pistols, but I'm passably tolerable with a rifle."

Sheriff Walsh looked a little nervous, and even Julian seemed to show a touch of strain.

After a moment, Dunphy said, "Kirkville, it seems, has just acquired a very interesting citizen."

"I didn't catch your full name," said Netfield.

"My full name is Sherrod Taunton Wingate," said Wingate.

"All right, Sherrod," said Netfield. "Maybe you'd like a rifle instead of a six-gun. Tell Efferson to give you the best one in stock."

"Yes, sir!" said Sherrod Taunton Wingate.

V

WINGATE ROLLED away toward Kirkville in the sheriff's buckboard and, a moment or two later, Julian and his two companions rode away at an easy rocking chair lope toward the distant pine-crested hills; Netfield was relieved at their departure. Quinty and Sheriff Walsh stepped inside the cabin and closed the door. Netfield was alone with Dunphy on the narrow porch.

After an instant, in tones of heavy intimacy, Dunphy said, "I'm afraid you've made a bitter enemy of Sheriff Walsh, Mr. Netfield."

"They're the kind to have, the bitter ones," said Netfield amiably. "The enemies that are bad are the friendly ones. No offense, Mr. Dunphy."

"I declare I'm unable to understand you," said Dunphy heartily. "Something seems to have upset you."

They took their horses from the rack and mounted. Their saddles were side by side, stirrup by stirrup.

"We must become better acquainted in Kirkville, sir," said Dunphy.

"No doubt we shall," said Netfield.

"*Adios*," said Dunphy with a flourish. "I'm headed for C Bar C."

"Then I'll ride along with you," said Netfield politely. "I, too, am headed for C Bar C."

Dunphy's big face flushed and hardened.

After an instant, he said, "Delighted to have your company."

Despite the fact that C Bar C was almost a little county in itself, the cluster of buildings which comprised its center, although large, was otherwise unimpressive. This was a working-ranch and showed it. Some of the buildings showed whitewash, some not; none of them bothered with paint. The buildings lay as though tossed, in the bend of a creek, in a salient of cottonwoods. To the north, in the general direction of Kirkville, rolled the rich prairie; to the south, toward distant badlands and stark mountains, lay, invisibly, Wingate's hard-proven homestead, now owned by Dunphy, and, beyond, 7 Diamond. Now, in the late afternoon sun, the blinding air seemed to burn with a metallic powder of incandescence.

Colonel Crewe had chosen his building site on a long abandoned emigrant road. On one side of the road were blacksmith shop, wagonshed, windmill and bunkhouse, cookhouse and barns; on the other, the ranch house. Behind the ranch house, over it, stood Hungry Butte.

Netfield and Dunphy dismounted before the blacksmith shop. It was about suppertime, and a few hands gathered around them. The C Bar C riders were all of high caliber. Colonel Crewe picked them with care and there were no finer lot of men west of the Dakotas. Netfield knew many of them personally, and all of them by sight. One of them said hospitably, "We're fixing to eat. Won't you join us?"

"Sorry," said Netfield. "But not this time. I'm seeing Mr. Colfax a moment, then I'm moving along."

Dunphy stared at him, but said nothing.

Netfield crossed the road, to the ranch house. It was a simple four-room cabin, built in the shape of a squared-U, of log, faced with cottonwood planking. This was Cimarron's choice of homes. At one end of the cabin was a door, and over it the Colonel had nailed a small neat sign: *Office*.

Netfield opened the door and entered.

It was a pleasant little office, with a few chairs and a rolltop desk. There was a rack of pigeonholes, stuffed with papers, and a shelf of ledgers. Elton Colfax stood in his undershirt, painting the windowsill with olive-green wagon paint.

Elton Colfax was C Bar C's kingpin. In Kirkville he was known inaccurately as the ranch's manager; actually, he was its foreman. He was famous in three counties for his energy, efficiency, and fanatical obsession with cattle. Dunphy was his immediate boss, and over Dunphy, of course, was Colonel Crewe.

Colfax was a chunky giant of a man with glossy black hair and a chiseled, too-handsome face already gone to dumplings of age at the corners of his jaw. Hard work and ability had made him a minor executive. He was range-born, and range-raised, and he liked to allude to these facts in a joking manner, as though they were handicaps he had outgrown. Netfield knew him only by sight; he had never, as far as he could remember, exchanged a single word with him. He had already painted the door, baseboard, and mantel shelf.

He wheeled majestically as Netfield entered.

"I'm George Netfield," Netfield said.

"I know," said Colfax. His voice was neither cordial nor hostile. "You own the Blue Banner."

He's trying to classify me socially, thought Netfield dryly. He doesn't want to snub a superior, or lower himself with an inferior.

After a pause, Colfax asked curiously, "What brings you here, Mr. Netfield?"

"I'm here to deliver a message," said Netfield. "Well, Dunphy pulled it off. He now owns the Wingate place."

Carefully, Colfax laid down his brush. "Is that supposed to mean something to me?"

Netfield looked impatient.

"Did Dunphy tell you this?" asked Colfax.

"He didn't have to tell me. I took part in it. When he shows you the papers, you'll see my name as one of the witnesses to the transfer. We made the deal at Quinty's less than an hour ago. Walsh and Julian and Dunphy and I."

Almost inaudibly, Colfax said, "What about Wingate? Did they fix him?"

"He's still alive."

"Well, I guess it makes no difference, really."

"Except to Wingate," said Netfield.

Colfax grinned. Changing the subject, he said, "How do you like my painting, Mr. Netfield?"

"Very spruce and high-toned."

"Isn't it, though," said Colfax. "I've always held you can't beat a nice olive-green for an office."

"I'll be moving along," said Netfield. "One thing more. I'd like to talk to Kruger before I go."

"Didn't Dunphy tell you?" said Colfax. "Kruger thought he'd better drift."

"To where?"

"You know Kruger. He never says. I'm sure surprised to find you mixed up in this, Mr. Netfield."

"I'm surprised to find myself mixed up in it," said Netfield. With a vague nod of farewell, he left the office.

Dunphy was standing in the golden glow of the setting sun, before the cookhouse. His questioning eyes took Netfield apart, piece by piece, but he said nothing. Netfield swung into his saddle, trotted his mare to the road, and headed north.

For the first two miles, until he was certain he had left C Bar C land behind him, he followed the road.

After a bit, he came to the mouth of a wash. Now he turned from the road into the wash and began a seemingly endless climb, for the gulch floor, rocky and uneven, sloped steeply upward. On either side of him, the tops of the eroded banks were tufted with tangled grass. Eventually the wash ended, and Netfield and his mount came out upon a high, open tableland.

There was sweet grass here, and a mountain stream, and at one edge of the little shelf a cluster of tilted, huge rocks. In the near distance below him, he could see the mustard-yellow road. To the south, the buildings of C Bar C, like dice, burned out in the brassy afterglow, and the surrounding sun-stained prairie faded to pale cinnamon.

Moving deliberately, Netfield picketed his mount behind the cluster of rocks, sat on his heels in a crevice, and waited.

The first horsemen came rolling up the road from C Bar C, two of them, in the last bronze light, men and mounts merging like frantic rubber toys. This, he knew, would without doubt, be Colfax and Web Dunphy. They came, and went, disappearing hell-for-leather toward the north, looking for George Netfield, but looking for him like a couple of lunatics.

The second group of horsemen came also from the south in a low, carelessly riding knot of perhaps eight men. They came not from C Bar C, but, as Netfield could see from his perch, from beyond it. And as they approached the C Bar C buildings from the south, they swung wide around them, bypassing them. These were 7 Diamond men, and Netfield watched them with a little chill. As Netfield had expected, they had received the word. They were like strange animals blending into the sage, blending into the gray, moonlit twilight. They tried to trail as they rode, but there was not sufficient light.

Now Netfield knew truly that there was a confederation marshaled against him.

At ten, he lay in the lush grass and slept until two. At two in the morning, he began a long, circuitous return to town.

He arrived in Kirkville about two in the afternoon.

The first man he spoke to was Andy Efferson, in front of his store on Main Street.

Efferson said, "Colonel Crewe's dead."

"Dead?" said Netfield, wiping his dust-caked lips with the back of his hand. "What do you mean? What happened?"

"He went into the pen that belongs to the Clover Butcher Shop. There were three mean bulls in it. He stumbled and it spooked them and they went for him. They broke his neck."

"There must have been a witness, to know that he stumbled."

"There was—one of his own cowboys. These things happen, George."

VI

As NETFIELD came along the boardwalk to the Blue Banner, he saw that its door was wide open for business, doorstopped with a case of empty beer bottles. Pleased and surprised, he entered. The Blue Banner's front room was dim, cool, and sedate. Its walls were tongue-and-groove pine, walnut-stained and waxed, Virginia style, rather than papered or painted. The walnut bar was short, blocky, and genteel; Netfield had bought it from a man who had bought it from a wrecked steamboat up on the Missouri River. The back bar was a tall mirror, highly silvered and simply framed, bare of all customary ornamentation such as locally famous poker hands, wisps of Cheyenne scalps, or chromos or dancing girls. The back bar shelf glistened with spirit bottles, and at the far end was a goldfish bowl filled with uncooked eggs beside a shaker of red pepper, the makings of a prairie oyster breakfast for queasy morning-after stomachs. The eggs that he had left had been brown. These were new eggs, snowy white. Wingate had replaced them.

Wingate, his yellow hair gleaming, a new grain sack about his waist as an apron, was behind the bar serving a drink to a prosperous back-country ranchman. He was being so solicitous, and intense, and so somehow threatening about it, that he was making the customer nervous.

The ranchman drank down and left. As he passed Netfield, he said, "Whew! I'm glad to see you back, George."

Netfield grinned.

Alone with Wingate, he said, "Thanks for opening shop for me. But I thought you said you didn't know how to tend bar."

"The customers are teaching me," said Wingate.

Cocking an eyebrow, Netfield said, "You trust them?"

"Yes, sir," said Wingate. "I trust them. I ask them what they want, and how much, and what it's supposed to cost, then serve them. While I'm serving them I give them a friendly smile and say offhand that I abominate a dishonest man. They say they do too. Some say it fast, some say it slow, and some even spill part of their drink, but they all say it. It's hard to put into words, but I have a feeling nobody's cheated me. By the way, did you hear about Colonel Crewe?"

"Yes. Yes, I did. Who was the cowboy that was with him?"

"No one seems to know."

"Then how do they know he was a C Bar C man?"

"Folks just figured he was. And when he rode up to the Antlers to report it, he was on a horse with the C Bar C brand."

"Up to the Antlers to report it? Is that the new sheriff's office?"

"He said he needed a drink."

"That's understandable," said Netfield. "What really happened, according to the story you heard?"

"I heard it two dozen times, and it was always just about the same. This cowboy was riding past the Clover pen and saw three bulls in it, waiting to be butchered. A farmer passing through had sold them to Dalton, the butcher. One of them looked like a mighty fine animal to the cowboy so he went around to Crewe's and told him he ought to buy it for the ranch. Crewe went with the cowboy back to the Clover pen to look it over. They got there just about dusk. Dalton had locked up for the night and gone home."

Netfield listened intently.

"Like I say," said Wingate, "it was growing dark when they got to the pen. The Colonel went inside the pen to get a better look. He stumbled, and the bulls went crazy and came at him. They stomped him and broke his neck. The hand dragged him out, but he was already dead."

Netfield nodded, and changed the subject. "Here's the situation. I'm likely going to be busy with a few outside things and I'm not sure how much time I'll be able to put in here at the Banner. You're doing fine. Shall we lock up, or do you want to keep open?"

"I'd like to keep open."

"Fine. But you're going to need help. There's a pretty nice fellow around town named McDonald we use as an extra now and then. Send out the word for him and he'll be around and give you a hand."

"Thank you, Mr. Netfield. I will."

Turning to leave, Netfield hesitated. Behind the bar, and leaning against it so that it projected a few inches above the bar top, was what could have been a broomstick draped with a cloth. If it was a broomstick, it was a mighty short one. There could be no doubt of it; it was a rifle. Wordlessly, Netfield pointed at it.

"My new Winchester," said Wingate happily. "And I forgot to thank you for it."

"There's a sawed-off shotgun beneath the bar and a forty-five by the cashbox," said Netfield. "I like to have weapons handy, but not so thunderation handy, pointing right in the customers' faces. You'll have to put that thing in the back room."

A mulelike stiffness came into Wingate's mouth.

In a soft voice, like the whisper of leather, he said, "I don't want to cross you, Mr. Netfield, but I can't do it. It would go agin all my natural elements. Like I told you before, a rifle is like a mother to me. Please don't separate us."

"I won't," said Netfield quietly. "Forget it."

Fatigued and moody, he left the Blue Banner and headed for the Jerome House.

He came to the Jerome House from the rear, because this was the shortest way, took an outside stairway to the second floor, and made his way down the dusty hall.

Netfield had two rooms connecting, at the front of the hall, by the main stairwell, numbers 7 and 8. Unlocking the door to 8, he entered his bedroom. The room was almost monastic in its simplicity and cleanliness. Moving slowly and accurately, as he always moved when he was exhausted, he stripped, bathed, shaved, and put on clean linen and broadcloth. Then, in his shirtsleeves, carrying his gun and cartridge belt loosely in the crook of his arm, he turned the big china knob in the connecting door and moved into 7.

Room 7 was Netfield's home, and he had decorated it at his own expense, and according to his own taste, to counteract the Blue Banner. Its St. Louis wallpaper was somber gray overprinted with green-and-gold medallions; it had stiff armchairs, a shiny black ramshorn sofa, and a three-foot plaster vase on the floor in a corner. Now, as he entered, the green blinds were pulled. As he stepped forward through the almost liquid halflight, he saw that Cimarron Crewe, in the deadest of black mourning, was sitting on his black sofa.

She arose, came to him, stood before him. He regarded her gravely.

He noted what he had missed before, her tense, restrained beauty, and then his mind wandered. This girl's relationship with her father had been particularly close and strong. He wondered what the death had done to her, what it was doing to her this very moment.

As she stood before him, she was ashen. He realized it was not only from grief, but also from anger.

In a tight voice, she said, "Web Dunphy and Elton Colfax have been to see me."

"They shouldn't have worried you in your moment of bereavement," said Netfield coldly.

"They say you're spreading stories about them. I've come to order you to stop."

"I have the stories to spread," said Netfield. "But I'm not spreading them." Absently, he buckled on his gunbelt.

From a wardrobe in the corner, he took a fresh square-skirted frock-coat and slipped it on. He was dead-tired, and had no desire to talk.

He stood for a moment, staring at her. Finally, he said, "I'm afraid I'd better tell you, and now. You're in trouble."

She scarcely listened.

"Miss Cimarron," he said. "In this country, cows are gold.

But a cow is practically worthless without a railroad car to ship it. Your father was the county's most influential and powerful man for one reason only: He owned the Kirkville Feeding Yards and negotiated its shipping contracts with the railroad. That feeding yard is the county's gateway to the outside world. Who controls it, controls the county."

Now he had her attention.

He said, "A group of men are in the actual process of taking over that power. My guess is that they have been building up strength for some time, taking advantage of your father's illness. Now he is gone. Now they will move in."

"How can they?" she scoffed. "I now own the business. And who are these men?"

"Dunphy is one of them, and Colfax," said Netfield. "Working with 7 Diamond."

He saw that as he spoke, he was becoming a loathsome creature in her eyes.

"You must break up this thing," he said.

Now she listened to him with contempt. After a moment, she said, "I've always felt you were a dangerous man, Mr. Netfield. How can you profit by these outrageous lies?"

Relentlessly, he went on. "I have a feeling this has been going on, down over the mountains in Bonnet County, for some time, through the Faynopolis Feeding Yards. But they've been getting more stolen stock than they can handle, stock from the great cattle empires down in Wyoming, perhaps. My guess is that they intend to move these stolen southern cows up to the Kirkville Feeding Yards, *where Dunphy can legalize them with forged bills of sale and ship them!* I believe 7 Diamond to be an outlaw hive, and nothing else. Southern cows, moved north by 7 Diamond men, will come through the pass, over 7 Diamond range, over C Bar C range, blessed on their way by Colfax, into the Kirkville Feeding Yards."

"Web Dunphy," she said, "was almost a brother to my father. Elton Colfax was almost a son to my father. And who are you?"

She walked to the door. "Leave us alone. All of us."

To her back, he said, "One thing more. Just for my personal satisfaction. Was your father a lunatic?"

Half turning, she glared at him, rage making her speechless.

"That, and only that," said Netfield, "would explain his final action. Would any sane veteran stockman expect to pick up a good bull in a butcher's pen? Even if this were so, would he go in the dark to inspect it?"

She wavered an instant, then said, "I suppose I should tell you the truth. Last evening, just after supper, my father was in his office and I was in the kitchen. My father came into me and said one of his hands was in the office. The hand had just ridden past the Clover pen and had seen some bulls in it. One of those bulls looked like C Bar C. They decided they'd better take a good look at it before they caused a rumpus. People are too quick of accusing a butcher of selling rustled stuff, and Dalton had a fine, honest reputation. They decided if anyone caught them looking, and it wasn't a C Bar C animal, they would use that other story. The story the cowboy used when he reported the accident."

"Who was the cowboy, by the way?"

"I don't know," she said. Indignantly, she added, "But he was someone my father liked and trusted."

When Netfield made no answer, she said, "There's no mystery about him. About half the town saw him when he reported the accident."

"You'd better get home and take a drop or two of laudanum," said Netfield gently. "You could use a little sleep."

After she had gone, he took his hat and headed for the courthouse and Sheriff Walsh.

VII

THE LATE afternoon sun, hanging low and red in the western sky, burned along the storefronts of Main Street as Netfield moved down the boardwalk, east from the Jerome House.

There were few horses at the rails, and those showed punishment from the heat. Now and then a hot breeze sprang up, gusty and desiccating, kicking up corkscrew dustdevils in the sunken roadway. At this time of day, the loafers' benches before the shops and offices were almost completely deserted. The very emptiness of the street made the three men before Gerhardt's Gunshop noticeable. They sat sprawled under the wooden awning, in the gray tissue-thin shade, ragged, bestial, venomous.

They were 7 Diamond men he had seen the day before at Quinty's road-ranch, the men who had been guarding Wingate. Their leader, the sinuous snake-chinned rider, was not with them.

They stared sleepily at Netfield as he advanced upon them, humped lazily to their feet, and slouched through the swing-door of an adjacent saloon.

They've come to town for me, Netfield thought. They're making their first open act. But this isn't the moment; they're not quite set.

He passed the saloon with scarcely a sidewise glance, and came to the Mockingbird Restaurant. Here he stopped for a moment, and gazed south, across the street, at the courthouse.

He felt his shoulder touched lightly from behind, and turned. The young waitress, Violet Archer, stood in the Mockingbird's doorway. Her pale, shiny face was distorted with worry. "How long have you known me, Mr. Netfield?" she asked.

"For almost two years," said Netfield. "Ever since you stole eighty-seven cents from your uncle's shuck mattress, and walked in from his farm, thirty miles through scrub and badlands, so you could live in a big city like Kirkville."

"There wasn't no need for you to mention all that," she said stiffly. "What I mean is, about the other night at the Antlers when I was with that Mr. Buttermilk Johnson. Do you think I'd have taken that brooch from him if I'd have known where it came from?"

"Not you," said Netfield gravely. "You're too careful."

She looked pleased. "That's right. And too honest. I just wanted you to understand. I like people to think well of me. Do you know a man from 7 Diamond, I think he's foreman there, named Julian?"

That was the snake-chinned man.

"I've met him," said Netfield.

"Well, you're going to meet him again. I served him a bowl of potatoes and a big steak with four eggs on it about an hour ago."

Netfield looked quizzical.

She said, "He ate at a back table with three other 7 Diamond men. I could hear them talking through the door to the kitchen. At five o'clock Sheriff Walsh is going out in the county to serve a paper and as soon as he's gone they're going to kill you. They're going to hunt you down and kill you."

Her pale face took on a look of genuine concern.

"Maybe," said Netfield, "I can put on an apron and sunbonnet and sneak out of town."

Now she looked jarred, and revolted. "You're joking."

After a moment, he asked, "Do something for me?"

"You bet."

"Go to the Blue Banner. Behind the bar you'll find a young fellow with yellow hair, Mr. Wingate. Tell him what you've told me. Then tell him to lock up the Banner, now, immediately, lock himself in the back room, and not go out on the street. Make an ugly face at him, and growl, and tell him these are strict orders."

"I don't like to make ugly faces at people, Mr. Netfield."

"Well, do it your own way," said Netfield. "But make him mind you. Unless you want him shot to dogmeat." He crossed the street to the courthouse.

The courthouse was of brick, two stories, the most prosperous-looking building on Main Street.

Netfield circled it to the rear, passing through the county

hitching-lot, and entered the building through a brick archway. He walked along a musty, brick-floored hall. The third door said OFFICE OF THE SHERIFF, and he turned in.

Two men were in the small, gray-painted room: Sheriff Walsh and one of his deputies, a man about whom Netfield knew little, a man named Cantrell. They were sitting across a table from each other, playing checkers, Cantrell big, hulking, oafish-looking, Walsh sly, furtive-eyed, lips smeared with tobacco drool. At the moment of Netfield's entry, the sheriff was making a move and he was making it in this manner: his hand extended over the board was flat, fingers glued together, with only the joint of his left thumb in sight, thumb tucked under, as his second finger made the move.

As Netfield walked in, he said, "I'm afraid your boss is cheating you, Mr. Cantrell. I come from where they play checkers for high stakes, and that's an old trick. While he's moving one man with his index finger, he's covering another with his palm, and moving it *too*, with his thumb."

Sheriff Walsh put his hands in his lap, and tried to bristle.

Cantrell said slowly, and with infinite insult, "When I want your advice, Mr. Netfield, I'll go to the Blue Banner and get drunk and ask it."

For the first time, really, Netfield studied the man. He was middle-aged, thin-haired, and pockmarked. He wore the clothes of a farmer, but it was well known that at one time he had been a topnotch cattleman. The terrible winter of 86-87 had bankrupted him. He had wandered in to Kirkville, lived from hand to mouth, and drifted into a deputyship.

Hesitating, Netfield said, "Excuse me."

"And I don't want your apology either," said Cantrell woodenly. "All I want is for you and everybody else to stay out of my affairs."

"Sheriff," said Netfield, "I want to report a case of justifiable homicide. As you've no doubt heard, several nights ago I shot a man known as Buttermilk Johnson in the wine room at the Antlers."

"You're durn right I heard."

"They didn't give Clyde Gilday an even break. They murdered him and robbed him, Spunky Martin and this Buttermilk Johnson."

"That might be so," conceded Sheriff Walsh. "Leastways the whole town's talking about that brooch. But how come you to slap him down that awful way and shoot him, though?"

"He was resisting arrest," said Netfield.

"Arrest?" said Sheriff Walsh. "What do you mean, arrest?"

"I was taking him in charge. Under the law, every citizen has a potential power of arrest."

Outraged, Sheriff Walsh said, "Not in my county! By golly! Why, I never heard the likes."

Cantrell said, "They tell me you and the sheriff met next day out at Quinty's road ranch. Why didn't you report it then?"

"It slipped my mind," said Netfield.

"Naturally," said Cantrell. "And besides it was justifiable."

"Exactly," said Netfield.

"This is a kind of busy afternoon for me," said Sheriff Walsh, his voice greasy with a sudden show of cordiality. "Shortly I got to ride out in the county and serve a paper. If you don't have nothing else on your mind I wonder if you'd take all this up with me later. I got to get ready for my trip."

"Before I leave," said Netfield. "I wonder if you'd satisfy my curiosity?"

"If I can," said Sheriff Walsh effusively. "Glad to, glad to."

"How does Web Dunphy pay you? Direct salary, or percentage?"

Sheriff Walsh's eye bugged. His face purpled and expanded. In a rain-barrel baritone, he said loudly, "He don't pay me no way at all. The county pays me."

There was an instant of stillness.

Cantrell broke it. He said, "There you are. You asked him and he told you. You had your curiosity satisfied. Now move along."

Netfield turned slowly and faced him. Quietly, he said, "Don't whip your trace chains at me too often, friend. I don't care for it."

Cantrell looked amused. "Fixing to arrest me, like you did this Buttermilk Johnson?"

"It shouldn't be too hard to do," said Netfield.

He wheeled, and left the room. As he passed through the door, he could feel the ice of Cantrell's eyes on his back.

Out in the corridor, he had just closed the door behind him when he heard the first shot. It was a rifleshot, muted by distance, and seemed to come from the direction of lower Main Street.

He put his ear to the panel beside him. Inside they must have heard it, too, but there was no stir of movement. Deliberately, the sheriff was refusing to take any action.

He broke into a lope along the brick flooring, passed through the archway and into the open, when distant pistols cut loose in ragged volleys. Running lightly, he circled the rear of the courthouse and came out into Main Street's broad roadway.

The boardwalk across the street was deserted, but every doorway sheltered a man or two, rancher, farmer, townsman, peering out, gawking cautiously southward.

In the center of the sun-baked road, about five yards from where Netfield drew to a halt, a strange bit of action was taking place.

Three men—Kirkville's doctor and two citizens—and a girl, Violet Archer, were lifting a man known as High Play, a 7 Diamond rider, from the ground. He was one of the filthy, leather-chapped apes that Netfield had seen on the street only a short time before.

As they lifted him, High Play threw back his head and screamed. Taking a second look, Netfield understood. High Play had been shot through the thigh, the bone apparently smashed, and they were trying to carry him off for medication.

Netfield asked, "Violet, what happened?"

"No one seems to know," said the girl.

With an air of innocence as thick as molasses, she left the others and joined him.

When she was standing breast-close to him, just under his chin, she began to speak, rapidly, almost inaudibly. "I went to the Blue Banner and told Mr. Wingate what you said. He spit on a whiskey glass, and brought it to a high shine on his shirtfront, and studied it, and I didn't think he'd heard me. Then he said, 'I can't allow none of that'. Then he took a dishrag off a rifle that was leaning by his pockets with cartridges, and went out on the sidewalk with me and locked the door."

His cheeks suffused, Netfield listening stonily.

"Well," she continued. "Then he said to me, 'I don't mean to be unmannerly, Miss Archer, but kindly light a shuck. I got to take care of four men before they take care of Mr. Netfield, and I don't want you messing me up!' "

"How did I know he was crazy?" said Netfield in savage self-reproach. There was harshness in his voice, and steely admiration.

"Then hell broke loose," said Miss Archer, and added modestly, "if you'll forgive the slang."

With lightning-quick phrases, she painted the sequence of events. On the south side of Main Street, across the road, across the railroad tracks, was a hole-in-the-wall saloon known as Ihlmann's. The cowpuncher, High Play, came out of Ihlmann's door into the blazing sunlight, picking his nose. He'd started across the roadway, angling toward the Antlers. When he'd reached the middle of the road, within easy range for his Colt, Wingate had called, "All right, gun-thrower. You've got one, use it."

High Play had said, "What's that? Why?"

"Because I'm going to break your leg," said Wingate, and did.

That had been the rifle shot Netfield had heard as he closed the sheriff's door. The volley of pistol shots which followed had been High Play, writhing in the dust, fanning at nothing.

Indianlike, Wingate had melted into an alley and vanished. Out of the Antlers, the other 7 Diamond men, Julian and his two companions, had steamed like hornets. They had yelled at High Play, High Play had yelled back, and they had avalanched into the alley, in pursuit, heading north.

"Those people in the doorways," said Netfield. "Looking down the street. What are they interested in?"

"That's where they are now," said Miss Archer. "All of them. That Julian and his men and Mr. Wingate. Down there across the street, in the Mayhew Lumberyard."

From the lumberyard itself, came nothing but silence.

Mayhew's lumberyard was like any other cowtown lumberyard, but much larger than the average. The lumber was decked in neat cubes, in random heights varying from three feet to fifteen feet. Between these cubical stacks of lumber ran a labyrinth of narrow passages. The place was a warren of corners, and turns, and elevations. Netfield could think of no deadlier place for a battle.

Now, as he gazed at it, knowing to enter it might well be suicide, he tried to plan a course of action. He could think of nothing.

"I'm going over and in," he said. "They've got the boy cornered."

"I don't think so," said Miss Archer. "That 'boy,' as you call him, nice as he is, scares me. I think he led them there on purpose. I think he's got *them* cornered."

"I'm going over and in," repeated Netfield. He went down the boardwalk and crossed the street.

A twenty-foot wide wagonroad, rutted and rock-hard, led from the street through a gateway, into the bowels of the yards. Netfield entered the yard, making no attempt at concealment, his bootsoles throwing up little cushions of dust as he walked. On either side of him was a broken wall of lumber, formed from the boxlike stacks. The silence was heavy and ominous. About him, somewhere, experts were stalking each other to death. Something seemed unnatural; then he realized that in the distance even Main Street was quiet, waiting breathlessly.

He had gone perhaps a dozen yards when the sound of the first shot snapped the air, a single unanswered rifle shot. That was Wingate's new Winchester. There was just the solitary crack, then once more silence.

Suddenly to Netfield's left, and in front of him, out of a passage and into the roadway, walked a 7 Diamond man. One hairy hand was splayed flat to his shoulder and through its fingers ran blood. His holster was gunless and his second hand, curled and empty, pawed at his stubbled cheek.

Eying him with interest, Netfield said softly, "Just go on down this road and through the gate. You'll find the doctor on Main Street."

The man stumbled away.

Two out of the picture, and two left, thought Netfield. The boy was not doing too badly at that.

But one of the two left was Julian. And Julian, if Netfield was any judge of humanity, was as dangerous as a rabid fox.

Now Netfield took his Colt from its leather and held it laxly at his knee.

Frowning, he entered the passage from which the wounded man had just emerged. It wasn't much to go on, but it was something. Cautiously, every sense alert, he moved quickly now, but noiselessly.

Here the stacks of lumber, some low, some high, paraded past him within easy touching distance. On either hand, he knew, lay the maze of trails. High overhead was the hot sun, but here it was for the most part gray and shadowy, and underfoot all sound was absorbed by bark and weeds. It was a world of bark, rats, lizards, lumber and weeds.

He passed the first intersection, passed the second, and was about to turn left into the third, when a racketing fusillade of pistol shots assaulted his eardrums, coming from directly overhead. He flattened himself against a lumberstack, and froze.

Once more the pistol shots came from above him. Not rapidly, but this time slowly, with deliberation, like the tolling of a funeral bell. Men shot that way when they were finishing a wounded animal.

Wingate, I have brought you to your death, thought Netfield. May you rest in peace.

He gazed above him, and saw nothing, and looked about him.

Out of the air dropped a sprig of wild grapevine, hitting the path and resting by his foot.

Once more he looked upward and now, to his unspeakable relief, he saw the smiling face of young Wingate, his lifeless yellow hair aglow in the sunlight.

"Up," whispered Wingate. "Climb up, and mighty quiet."

Netfield climbed the stack of lumber and, like Wingate, lay prone on the hot planks.

Now he saw to his surprise that it had been Wingate, himself who had cut loose with the pistol shots, for beside him, by his knee, lay the old .45 from the Blue Banner cashbox.

And instantly he saw the great strategy the boy had played, played from the beginning. He was amazed and a little frightened at its eerie trickery. Wingate had planned this before he had left the Blue Banner. He had shot High Play, publicly, to advertise his rifle. He had led his pursuers into his lumberyard trap (and shot one who had doubtless been careless) entirely for this single, great moment.

Somewhere, at this instant, the 7 Diamond men, separated, tense as cats, were on the prowl. They had heard the death knell of pistol shots. They would be coming to investigate, coming warily, but still coming.

This pile of lumber was the highest in the vicinity, about twelve feet above the earth. From the elevation, Netfield could see foreshortened passages and the muddled stacks of lumber. He breathed silently, through open mouth, and

waited. Wingate waited, too, his rifle resting comfortably a-
gainst his cheek.

Abruptly, a man appeared, Julian's companion. He appeared below them, scarcely a dozen yards away, from a
passage mouth. He held two guns, walked almost mincingly
in his great caution, and moved his lips as though he were
in an argumentative dream.

Netfield tensed. In the softest of whispers, Wingate said,
"As pretty as he is, we're going to have to pass him by. Keep
your shirt on."

When it happened, it happened so quickly that Netfield
could scarcely comprehend it.

Deep in a passageway, a good eighty feet away, a patch
of color moved in the shadows, a patch of cloth that seemed
hardly as large as a man's hand, and Wingate shot.

A man creeping in a low crouch now thrashed upward in
an arch of pain—Julian—and Wingate shot again. Lifeless,
Julian slammed to earth.

The 7 Diamond rider just below them pounded away in
panic. He was fully in their view as he fled, rolling and
clicking and rattling in near hysteria.

"We'll leave him go," said Wingate thoughtfully. "My
pappy said it never hurts to always let one go."

They descended to the bark-floored earth.

"Ambushing," said Wingate, "is like anything else, I
guess. It helps to have a gift for it."

"And you have a gift for it," said Netfield.

"Yes," said Wingate. For a split instant, he seemed simply
childlike and honest. "At least that's what my kin say back
in Tennessee."

"And they should know," said Netfield.

Wingate echoed, "And they should know."

VIII

IT WAS A LITTLE after four-thirty when Netfield and Wingate
left the lumberyard. Up and down Main Street, people stared

at them but said nothing. Wingate returned to the Blue Banner; Netfield, passing the Antlers, walked east.

After a bit, not far from the edge of town, he came to a small false-fronted building set in a weedy lot. Over its door a big sign read THE CLOVER BUTCHER SHOP. There was no one in sight, which was just as well, for he was uninterested in either the shop or its proprietor. A path ran through the weeds to the rear of the building, and he followed this path.

Behind the shop were the sheds: woodshed, slaughtering and dressing shed, and smokehouse. Here, too, there was no one in sight. He continued onward past the sheds, and the ground, sloping gently downward, brought him into a small, uninhabited hollow.

It was a desolate spot, surrounded by a circle of scrub and clumps of saplings, and seemed a hundred miles from Main Street. In the center of the hollow was a small octagonal pen of oak planks; this was the Clover's holding pen for animals marked for slaughter. At the moment it held nothing but a scrawny calf.

Netfield paused and looked about him. He was interested not in the pen, itself, but in the surrounding terrain.

He got his bearings, and figured them out in relation to the Crewe home. When Colonel Crewe and the cowhand had come to this place, they had certainly come by the shortest and most convenient route, and not by Main Street. The Crewe house lay five blocks northwest; therefore, it was likely that the Colonel and his companion had come into the hollow from that direction. Netfield passed the pen, crossed the hollow, and started his search.

He was searching for a clump of scrub, or other shelter, close to the pen, but not too close, a spot isolated but not suspiciously isolated.

It took him twenty minutes to find it.

In a little cavern of branches, with a footpath running through it, he found it. First he saw only four rotted leaves, upturned. Then, examining the earth more minutely, building

it up mark up mark, he reconstructed the scuffle. There had
been a scuffle here; no, more than a scuffle, a thrashing,
violent, life-or-death fight. A tiny sparkle of gilt blinked up
at him from a patch of slimy toadstools. He uncovered it
more fully, and picked it up.

It was a fragment of watch chain perhaps four inches
long. It was a valuable chain, of soft gold, and its links were
fashioned in the ornate styling known as Babylonian. It had
been ripped apart, unconsciously, no doubt, and with great
muscular fury. This was Colonel Crewe's watch chain.
Here, in this leafy cavern, he had fought futilely against
cruel hands deliberately breaking his neck.

He had been killed here, then put into the pen.

Now, with bent head, Netfield followed the path to the
northwest, in an effort at backtracking.

There were many tracks, large and small, new and old,
clear and dim. But the track he was looking for could not
be confused with any of these. He was almost out of the
hollow when he found it. It was but a single imprint,
shadowy and ghostly, almost nonexistent, but undeniable.
The imprint of an Apache moccasin.

Kruger.

He hesitated a moment, wondering what to do, whether to
return to Main Street or continue on to the Crewe home.

Brooding and unhappy, he decided to continue on to the
Crewe home.

Cimarron Crewe was on her front porch, in a great fan-
backed wicker chair. She looked pallid, grief-ravaged, but
utterly in control of herself. Netfield turned down the walk.
He came up to the porch steps, and stopped at their base,
resting his foot on the second step, and his forearm on his
knee. For a moment they looked at each other, neither
speaking.

Finally, he said, "Last night, when your father died, a
cowpuncher came here to the house and told him about

the animals in the Clover pen. Then they walked down to the pen together. Is that right?"

"Yes."

"Walked?"

"Yes."

"But the puncher had a horse. He *rode* up to the Antlers and told his story." Netfield waited, then added, "Where was the horse?"

"It was here," said Cimarron. "Right there at the hitching block."

"So he came back and got his horse and rode to the Antlers and told his story. Why didn't he report it to you? You were the one most vitally concerned."

For a moment, she faltered. "I hadn't thought of that. I was so shocked I didn't think of that. I guess he didn't tell me because he hadn't the heart to."

"He didn't tell you," Netfield said, "because he wanted to make his report impersonally and burn out . . . haul his freight. If he'd hold you, he might have been detained, out of seeming politeness."

"I don't believe it," she said. "I'm not enjoying this conversation."

"Nor I, either," said Netfield. "The man's name was Kruger."

"It might very well have been Kruger," she said listlessly. "Kruger is one of C Bar C's top hands."

"Was," said Netfield. "He's no longer there."

From his vest pocket, he took the length of watch chain. He handed it to her. "This was your father's, wasn't it?"

She clutched it, and nodded.

Briefly, he told her where and how he had found it.

"Kruger," he said bleakly, "lured your father to that place, at that time, so he could kill him in a manner that would look like an accident."

Now she became angry. "He couldn't have. He was a new man at C Bar C, but he worshipped my father."

"Sort of a stepson?"

Bewildered, she said, "What do you mean?"

"Well," said Netfield, "if Dunphy was like a brother to your father, and Colfax a son, then maybe Kruger was like a stepson."

"I have a headache," she said, and he felt it might well be true. "You're a dangerous and perhaps a wicked man. I want no more conversation with you. Will you please go."

"Yes," said Netfield. "Of course. But first will you please answer this for me. How did that little piece of watch chain get buried among the toadstools and saplings, a good seventy feet from the pen?"

"It got there in some very natural way," she said calmly. "When my father's body was taken from the pen, a great crowd of milling people gathered. Maybe some child picked it up and carried it there and dropped it."

"Of course," said Netfield. "Now I wonder why I didn't think of that."

He bowed goodbye, set his black hat at an angle across his brow, and started down the walk for town.

"Didn't I hear some shooting a while ago?" she said. "Coming from the direction of the lumberyard?"

"I thought I heard it too," said Netfield confidentially.

He had supper alone at the Mockingbird. An hour and a half had passed since the battle, and in that hour and a half literally dozens of ranchers and townsmen spoken to Netfield of it, and expressed their judgment on it. Kirk County, even after all these years, never failed to amaze Netfield. Here was the community's popular judgement on the affair: Wingate had provoked High Play before he shot him, but he had done it fairly, giving him fair warning. It was only natural for Julian and his 7 Diamond men to wish to avenge the injury to High Play, in fact such a course was their duty. However, three 7 Diamond men against one Wingate was unfair; natural, and impulsive, but unfair. Nevertheless, however, on the other hand, Wingate had managed to come out of it safely. Therefore, taking all things into consideration, it had just been another interesting afternoon. Nobody was actually guilty of anything.

Violence and death made some men ravenously hungry. Upon Netfield, they acted adversely. Pushing back his chair, leaving his big supper practically untouched, he went stiffly out into the pre-dusk of the town.

The evening sky was as clear as a fishbowl covered with rose-bronze foil and there was no human in sight along the boardwalk, for this was the supper hour. Deliberately and gravely, like a gentleman enjoying an after-supper stroll, Netfield walked west along Main Street.

The stores thinned out, and gaped with vacant lots, and gave away at last to a line of dwindling, squalid cabins. The setting sun was a disc of cherry silk when he passed the town's corporation line and came eventually to the loading chutes. A sign on a rambling, unpainted building said: THE KIRKVILLE FEEDING YARDS. COL, CREWE, PROP.

He paused for a moment, gazing moodily about him, seeing everything now with new insight.

The property was truly mammoth; it was practically a small world in itself. Along the railroad tracks were the chutes. Flanking the chutes were the pens; the seemingly endless pens, loading pens, large and small, square and octagonal, like a tremendous lateral slice of honeycomb. The business aspects of this establishment, Netfield knew, presented more facets than he had fingers. There were the county shipping contracts and negotiations with the railroad. There was the feeding of stock and holding of stock, both cows and horses; the buying and selling of hay and grain; the buying and settling of stock by the yard itself, by contract, by arrangement, by auction. There were the endless negotiations and mediations between ranchers, traders, dealers, speculators, and reputable Eastern buyers. It was a business that walked a perpetual tightrope between great profits and financial calamity. It was Kirk County's heart, its very portal to the outside world.

Walking unhurriedly, cloudy with rage, Netfield turned

from the path to the building. Bypassing the front door, he knocked on a door at the rear.

A muffled voice yelled, "Come in!", and he entered.

This was Web Dunphy's bedroom, and it was a pigsty. In one corner was a dented iron bed, with a nestlike tangle of filthy bedclothes. The floor was clay and dirt encrusted and littered with everything from a soiled lavender silk sleeve garter to dry spongelike quids of discarded chewing tobacco and mouldy peachseeds. Dunphy stood by a washstand, before a mirror, his head thrown back. He was sawing wild hairs out of his nostrils with a little goldplated penknife. The glossy purple lids of his froglike eyes were half closed in concentration. His stockman's boots were shined, he wore an expensive plaid suit, and his shirt was snowy and immaculate. In a general way, the overall picture was not new to Netfield. You could almost say it was a frontier phenomenon. He had seen many a Western dandy emerge fastidious from just such squalor.

"Good evening," said Netfield mildly.

Dunphy closed his penknife and turned. "Well, howdy," he said. "Howdy." His voice suddenly inflated with an excess of cordiality. "Take a chair, George. Sit down."

"George?"

"Mr. Netfield. I mean make yourself comfortable."

When Netfield simply stood there in silence, Dunphy said effusively, "Can I do something for you?"

In deep thought, Netfield blew out his lips, soundlessly, and sucked them in. Finally, he broke his silence. He said, "I don't want Julian of 7 Diamond buried in the same cemetery with Clyde Gilday."

Dunphy looked perplexed. "But why tell me? I scarcely knew the man."

"Now that I've thought it over," said Netfield. "I don't want him even buried in Kirkville."

"Then you'd better talk to 7 Diamond, Mr. Netfield," said Dunphy. He tried to sound reasonable. "I don't know where you got the idea that this Julian and I—"

"Who's going to try for me next?" asked Netfield. "Kruger?" Maintaining his shell of joviality with difficulty now, Dunphy said, "Dammit, something just occurred to me. There's a possibility, a bare possibility, that I may be able to do you a favor. With Colonel Crewe's unhappy misfortune, I've taken over the management of the Antlers. Now, to be perfectly frank, it's a kind of business a little out of my line. It strikes me you'd be a much better man for the position. Maybe if I'd talk to Miss Cimarron she might—"

Cutting him off curtly, Netfield said, "Know why I'm here, Dunphy?"

The Dunphy that answered was a completely new Dunphy to Netfield. He was quiet, hard, and competent. He said, "No, Mr. Netfield. I've been wondering."

"In my opinion, you sent 7 Diamond to get me this afternoon and they misfired. I thought I'd give you another chance. I thought if I stood before you, in person, the sight of me might tempt you."

Veiled and dangerous, under perfect control, Dunphy said, "First, I'll repeat: I don't know what you're talking about. Then, I'll add this. I don't tempt. I doubt if you ever met a man just like me, Mr. Netfield."

"According to *you*. According to *me*, you're no different than any other riffraff. No different, say, than Buttermilk Johnson or Julian."

"And you may not believe it," said Dunphy placidly. "But I don't scare, either."

"Well, anyway," said Netfield, turning to leave. "I gave you your chance."

"A real smart man never plays chances," said Dunphy.

Main Street was settling down for the evening when Netfield returned to town. There was a flush of stragglers on the walk, women bent on after-supper trading, children playing, a few citizens picking their teeth. A stage traveler, seeing Kirkville at this hour, would think the town unusually cozy and friendly. The door to Efferson's store was

open and, in the yellow light of a lamp on the counter, Efferson was removing candles from a candlebox and stacking
them in a bin. Netfield swung into the store and drew up
before his friend.

Looking up, Efferson said, "George." He smiled a quiet
smile of friendship, and added, "I was just getting ready to
close for the day and look you up. We're taking a little trip
tomorrow."

"Can't do it," said Netfield. "Can't leave Wingate alone
at the Banner. Trip to where?"

"Miss Cimarron is riding out to C Bar C in the morning,
and wants me to escort her. I want you to come along."

"No," said Netfield. Quizzically, he added, "Why you?"

"I've been a close friend of the Crewes for a long time.
The Colonel, by the way, was greatly misunderstood."

Netfield witheld comment.

"In my opinion," said Efferson, "you and Miss Cimarron
represent the best the county has to offer. I want to see
you together, and know you stand together."

Quietly, Netfield gave Efferson a quick review of the con-
versations he had had with her, the conversation in the
hotel, the one on her porch. He told him, too, of the finding
of the watch chain.

Efferson listened, distressed.

After a moment, he said, "Be patient with her, George.
Come along with us."

"Very well," said Netfield decisively. "Actually, I have a
little business out that way myself. I'll meet you on the
road, and we'll see how things work out."

"Good enough," said Efferson. "You're doing the right
thing."

The lobby of the Jerome House was beginning to stir with
evening activity. As Netfield entered, the clerk came forward to meet him. Nudging Netfield into a corner, con-
spiratorially, he handed him a telegram. "It come about a

hour ago," he said. "But I declare I can't make no sense
of it."

The wire, scribbled on wrapping paper in the station-
masters' flowery hand, said: *Figure just about now you can
use a good hired hand. Am sending along a friend. Smith.*
It had been sent from Skinners Junction, New Mexico.

"You see," explained the clerk. "You ain't no farmer and
don't need no hired hand. That's the point that befuddles
us, ain't it? It must be meant for some other Netfield."

Smith, thought Netfield? Who in the world is Smith?

Only one Smith had come into his life recently, and that
was Buck Smith, the gunman. Buck had said he would head
for New Mexico. It was Buck, all right, and he was sug-
gesting that Netfield retain a professional gunslinger.

Quick, with pencil on the back of an envelope, Netfield
dashed off an answer: *Buck Smith, Skinners Junction, New
Mexico. As a friend of mine has just said you must have
wrong Netfield as I don't hire anyone in your line of work
under any circumstance whatever. Therefore am rejecting
offer. Thanks just the same and good luck. Netfield.*

"If we don't know him," said the clerk. "How do we
know his line of work?"

"We put that in to be polite," said Netfield.

"I'll send a boy over to the station with it," said the clerk.
"But it's going to cost you a lot of money. Why didn't you
just say, 'no'?"

"I meant a little more than no," said Netfield.

IX

ABOUT FOUR MILES south of Kirkville, a few yards from the
road, was a seep-spring and a clump of alders; here, next
morning, Netfield waited. Beside him, on short picket, was
his second-best saddle horse, Velvet. Any owner other than
Netfield would have long ago disposed of Velvet for her
hide and hooves. All her characteristics were bloodcurdling,

and all but one bad. She was a ravenous eater (celluloid collars, corral rails, human ears); she was a kicker and a crusher; she was suicidal when the mood came over her. These were just a few of her blemishes. Netfield loved her for her speed. In a race or a chase, she poured her natural viciousness into muscularity and was almost unbeatable. Now, happily, she munched grass and bark, and once, as Netfield glanced at her, she seemed to be cracking a nut or eating a small rock. About ten forty-five, a puff of dust came down the road from the north and materialized into two riders, Cimarron and Efferson.

Netfield rode from the clump of alders and intercepted them. Cimarron sidestepped her mount in startled hostility.

Angrily, she said, "Why were you waiting for us?"

Netfield ignored her. To Efferson, he said severely, "Will you explain to me, sir, why you are following me?"

"We're following no one," said Cimarron, outraged.

"Oh, I see," said Netfield pleasantly. "You mean *I'm* following *you.*"

"No," said Cimarron. "You were ahead of us on the road, so naturally we're following you. What I mean is we're not following you intentionally."

"I see you are changing your story," said Netfield graciously. "I'm happy to accept your apology."

"I'm not apologizing for anything whatever," said Cimarron. "And you very well know it."

Suavely, Andy Efferson said, "We're heading out to C Bar C, George. Where are you heading?"

"To Quinty's, among other places," said Netfield.

"Then we're all going in the same direction," said Efferson. "Why don't you join us?"

Netfield cocked an eyebrow at Cimarron, and waited politely.

She hesitated, then said, "The roads are public property."

"Thank you," said Netfield gravely. In a hoarse, audible whisper to Efferson, he said, "Now there's an invitation I shall always treasure."

All morning they moved southward, at a steady easy pace along the dusty road, across the flats, past alkali pools, past sepia, sun-burnt buttes, through rich grazing lands. At noon, they stopped by a sweetwater stream, in tree-shade, and had dinner. There had been little talk on the road, and there was little talk at dinner. Netfield had brought six sandwiches, three ham and three cheese, which they shared with him in roadside courtesy. Formally, he accepted food from Cimarron's hamper. He also brought three bottles of lemon soda, which he cooled in the stream while they ate.

When they had finished their meal, and were drinking the lemon soda, Cimarron said, "You appear to be quite an eater when traveling, Mr. Netfield. Six big sandwiches."

"I always like to go prepared," said Netfield. "What I don't eat, my little mare, Velvet, will."

They turned, all of them, and looked at the shaggy, tough little mare.

"And the lemon soda," said Cimarron. "Three bottles. Just three bottles even. Does she like lemon soda too?"

"Not the soda itself," explained Netfield. "She despises lemon soda. But she loves the bottles. She finds them very agreeable crunching."

"Now I know all this wasn't arranged," said Cimarron. "Your joining our party by accident and all your food and drink dividing up among us so evenly, but when you stop to think about it, you'll have to admit it's a remarkable coincidence."

"Coincidence is the mother of invention," said Netfield profoundly.

"Well," said Andy, grinning. "We'd better move on. We've got a long way to go."

Two hours before sundown, they reached Quinty's. The little cabin road-ranch seemed deserted. Its whitewashed walls gleamed in the heat, and a cloud of gnats tumbled beneath its dirt eaves. Its porch was empty and its yard was empty, and its only window was shuttered. When Netfield tried its door, he found it locked. He called, "Quinty!" but got not even a whisper of an answer.

He's inside, all right, Netfield decided. He saw me coming. He heard about Julian, and a few other things, and he wants none of me.

They led their mounts to the rear and watered them, and once more took the road south.

A half mile south of Quinty's was a midget butte, its cracks and crevices sprouting saplings, and here the road forked. The main road continued to C Bar C, and the smaller road, scarcely a wagon trail, led to the foothills.

Here at the fork Netfield said goodbye.

"Goodbye, Mr. Netfield," said Cimarron.

Netfield studied her. She wasn't unfriendly, but she wasn't exactly friendly either.

Gently, Andy Efferson said, "As you guessed, Miss Cimarron, this ride was arranged. But it was I who arranged it, not George. I wanted you to know him better. He has your best interests at heart. I want you to trust him."

"I like Mr. Netfield," she said quietly. "I realize now that I like him. But I want nothing whatever to do with him."

Andy persisted. "Why not?"

"For one thing," she said simply. "He frightens me."

Netfield was appalled.

"Can't you see it, Andy?" she said exasperated. "Can't Kirk County see it? This is a frighteningly dangerous man."

"He's no different from any other man," said Andy Efferson amiably. "Except that he lives by his principles."

"So does a Sioux war party," she said softly.

Netfield nodded a curt farewell, touched his hatbrim, and turned his mount into the side trail.

Soon he was in tangled scrub and greasewood. An hour later, he swung right, and was before long in a country of low hills threaded with miniature valleys of rich bottomland. At the most brilliant part of the day, a half-hour before sunset, he came to Wingate's homestead and cabin.

He sat his saddle for a long three minutes and studied it

before he dismounted. It was a tidy little place, well kept, and the land about it was rich and carefully cultivated. Wingate was as good a farmer as he was a rifleman. When Web Dunphy stole it from him, he must have stolen his heart's blood.

The tiny cabin was of well-selected logs, straight-grained and squared. There was a pole corral, a small log barn with a lean-to workshop, and, a short distance away, halfway up a wooded hillside, a log springhouse. There must have been a few horses and pigs and milch cows, too, but Dunphy or someone had confiscated them.

Warily, Netfield entered the cabin's single room. There was a bunk against one wall, a packingbox table in the center of the room, a good fireplace, and a whiskey barrel chair. On the floor lay chicken bones and chicken feathers, and in a corner, where they had been tossed, lay the feet, viscera, and heads of four chickens. On the floor, also, lay empty food cans, tomatoes, and pork and beans, opened crudely with a jackknife. By the head of the bed stood six empty pint gin bottles.

Netfield felt the hearthstone. It was cold.

Painstakingly, he searched the room, and found nothing further.

Wingate would never had fouled his immaculate cabin with feathers and chickenheads and empty tin cans. Nor could Wingate be a bed-drinker. This cabin had been used by a stranger, and for some time. And that stranger had killed and dressed Wingate's chickens *indoors*.

Indoors, because he was in hiding.

And who could safely hide between 7 Diamond and Colfax at C Bar C but a friend of Web Dunphy's?

Once more Netfield looked around him. Somewhere was the link he needed, the evidence which might destroy the entire conspiracy. And still he found nothing.

He went outside, into the glare of the setting sun, and glanced about him, his eyes traveling in quartering circles like a huntsman's.

Analytically, he considered the matter.

The man had hidden out in the cabin. He'd slept indoors, eaten indoors, even slaughtered his chickens indoors, out of sight of passersby or prying eyes. *But he'd have to have water.*

Netfield's gaze rose to the springhouse on the hill, and he ascended the path. As he climbed, he kept his eyes on the path for sign.

He found the sign inside the springhouse itself. The springhouse was a small cubicle of cottonwoods. At one end was the shallow pit which was the spring, carefully lined by Win· gate with shale. On either side were shelves with milk and butter crocks. In the moist ground beside the spring was a kneeprint and a single footprint.

It was a footprint of a moccasin. A big, splayed moccasin.

Netfield smiled bleakly. This was it. Kruger had been hiding here. Working for Dunphy, he had been hiding in Dunphy's newly acquired homestead. This was the tie that Netfield had hoped for, the tie between Dunphy and Kruger.

Near his shoulder, clinging to the bark of a cottonwood log, was something that looked like a little wad of cotton, or possibly a cocoon. Netfield broke it free, and smelled it. Soap. Dried lather. Kruger had shaved here, too, and wiped his razor on the bark. There was no doubt now. That moccasinprint was Kruger's. He was probably the only white man in the county who wore moccasins. And Indians didn't shave.

As he swung into Velvet's saddle, and headed northward, he realized he had simply a confirmation of his conviction and little more—nothing really to convince anybody, certainly not Cimarron, probably not even Andy. Anyone could wear a moccasin, Cimarron would say; and even if it were Kruger's, how did that prove connivance with Web Dunphy? Kruger had likely found an empty cabin and taken it over.

"The point is," Netfield could say. "The important point

is that I expected that moccasinprint on that homestead, *and found it.* I defy you or anyone else to repeat the performance anywhere in the county, at any spot of your own choosing."

"You are building much on nothing at all," she could argue.

But the time was long past for words or argument.

That night he slept in a little hollow black in shadow beneath a cupped ceiling of interlocking tree branches. Three times he awakened and changed Velvet's picket to new grazing, for he loved horses and thought always of their welfare. With the first shell-pink smudge of dawn he ate, and headed once more northward.

He reached C Bar C at seven o'clock, timing himself to arrive just after breakfast.

Cimarron, Andy, and Elton Colfax were standing by the ranch house steps and Colfax, in all his mail order finery, was knocking himself out being charming and impressive.

Velvet came up to them in an easy fox trot, and came to a stop, and Netfield said, "Good morning, all."

No one but Andy seemed pleased to see him.

Velvet bit a fly-bite on her hind leg, then put on one of those remarkable, always new, always unexpected shows which so endeared her to Netfield. This time, it was Colfax she honored.

She seemed suddenly to see him, and be fascinated by him. Out came her big neck, pointed at Colfax as though it were a cannon, and her bleary eyes seemed to pop. Her gigantic head swayed a little, then dipped. Starting at the ground, raising her head slowly as though it were elevated by pulleys, she inspected him: boots, pants, vest, shirt, and face. When she came to his face, her rubbery lips went back over her teeth and she nickered derisively.

Cimarron smiled, but Colfax darkened in anger, and stepped back.

"What's wrong with that polecat?" rasped Colfax.

"She's an old Pinkerton mare," lied Netfield pleasantly. "She doesn't like thieves."

Andy Efferson grinned stiffly, and tried to divert the insult. "You say she doesn't like beeves?"

"Not beeves," said Netfield, speaking clearly. "Thieves."

There was a moment of utter silence.

"Get down from that saddle," said Colfax numbly. "And take off that gunbelt."

Netfield stood in his stirrups, in the process of dismounting. Cimarron, standing by his knee, grasped him about the waist with blunt, firm hands and reseated him on his leather.

"We'll have none of that," she said.

Savagery and fury had wiped all handsomeness from Elton Colfax's face. He no longer looked like a Greek god. His cheeks were puffed and bloated with rage, his dimples were ghastly crevices, and his eyes became the eyes of a rabid pig.

"Saved by a woman," he said when he could speak. "The great Mr. Netfield, saved by a woman."

"That's right," said Netfield agreeably. "And it's a very pleasant sensation."

"I'll see you again," said Colfax.

"That would be very kind of you," said Netfield.

Two punchers came from the direction of the corral, leading Cimarron's and Andy's horses. They mounted, and with Netfield, rode from the ranchyard. Cimarron, and even Andy, seemed shaken by Colfax's frenzy. No one, however, had anything to say.

The ranch gate lay a mile from the buildings. As they passed through it, Netfield said, "He wasn't too pretty, was he, Miss Cimarron? I'll wager there was an Elton Colfax you never saw before."

A little tremulously, she said, "You called him a thief."

"What else could I call him? But that wasn't what drove him crazy. It was because I named him for what he is, before you."

After a moment, she said, "You provoked him deliberately. So that he would show himself before me in his worst light."

"In a bad light, but not his worst. I thought it might educate you."

"Well, it didn't," she said coldly. "It was a waste of time."

"I'm afraid it was," said Netfield.

For an instant, but only an instant, she seemed confused and worried.

"I don't understand you," she said. "What will you get out of all this?"

"Experience, for one thing," said Netfield. "And maybe an ounce or so of lead."

Night had fallen when they reached Kirkville. Cimarron and Efferson parted from Netfield at the courthouse, and headed toward the Crewe home. Netfield stabled Velvet at the livery barn and made his way to the Jerome House. As he entered the lobby, the nightclerk called to him.

"Mr. Netfield. A telegram."

Netfield turned to the desk. The telegram, written by the stationmaster in soft pencil on the back of a pink handbill, said:

> Received your wire too late. Article mentioned is already on its way. Nothing can stop it now. Best of luck to you. Your friend B. Smith.

Netfield was torn between amusement and annoyance. The article Bucky Smith was sending, he knew, was a professional gunfighter to assist him. Bucky meant well, was trying to do him a favor, Netfield knew, but if there was one thing Netfield wanted no traffic with, it was a hired gun.

But all that can be taken care of when he arrives, thought Netfield. I'll thank him, pay him a little something for his trouble, and fire him.

X

THE NEXT few days passed quietly, and in the very vacuum there was to Netfield a sense of growing tension. For one

thing, Kirkville, always hot at this season, underwent an almost unendurable increase in temperature as fiery desert
air moved in upon it, blanketing it, suffocating it. Chickens
were prostrated in the dust with spread, helpless wings, and
the mouths of dogs hung open, as though from fractured
jaws. Clapboards along Main Street seemed to warp in the
sun's blaze as leather curls upon a stove. In this cauldron
of fierce weather, 7 Diamond came to town.

They came quietly. First in the form of a straggler or
two, then in groups of increasing size and frequency.
Before any except Netfield and Efferson and Wingate realized
it, they were a fixture. They came first to Piano Street,
seeped unnoticeably across the railroad track to Main Street,
and soon seemed always to have a gun or two on hand,
night or day, somewhere.

Up and down Main Street, in the shops and saloons, these
leathery animals of Dunphy's became well known, not disliked. They spoke in courteous mumbles, and were woodenly
polite.

They had come to take over the town, Netfield knew.

They had come, too, for him—but they held off. They
held off, waiting patiently for the proper opportunity. For
their own safety in the assassination, perhaps, certainly for
anonymity. His death was of primary importance to Dunphy,
but his death under improper circumstances could do 7
Diamond (and therefore Dunphy) much public harm.

Wingate was constantly in Netfield's vicinity these days,
as an uninvited bodyguard, behind him, before him, across
the street from him, always carrying his Winchester. And
after a bit, the Winchester itself caused comment among the
citizenry, and puzzlement.

At the same time, Netfield was sure the talk helped greatly in preserving his life. For he was convinced of one thing:
Wingate worried the 7 Diamond gunhands. This innocent-
faced, serious young Tennessean was beyond their comprehension. He carried his rifle in his hand as a carpenter might
carry a saw, or as a housewife might carry a pair of scissors,

as an unconscious tool. They were themselves brutal, and could understand brutality, but he was without brutality. Even the worst of them, however, had somewhere in them a faint streak of humanity. But Wingate apparently, was without humanity. And that, Netfield decided bleakly, was what worried them.

Yes, this time when they hit—unless they hit in desperation—they would hit safely and properly. They couldn't afford another spectacle like the lumberyard disaster.

These tense hot days, Netfield combed the town painstakingly, asking questions about Kruger, attempting to materialize a phantom. A surprising number of people remembered this man. Piece by piece, Netfield built up a meticulous picture. Kruger was about twenty-eight, rawboned, big, slumpshouldered. Everywhere, too, he had left the same memory—the impression that he was utterly vicious.

One morning about noon, Netfield was in the Blue Banner, his foot on the rail, talking to McDonald, the reserve barman, when Wingate came in from the street with his Winchester, and joined them.

McDonald eyed the rifle and Wingate, then Netfield, and said, "This has been going on for a week now. Up to now I've held my tongue. But last night at supper I talked it over with Nora. We think you're in some kind of bad trouble, Mr. Netfield, you and Sherrod, and we want to help."

"We're in no trouble," said Wingate.

"Where would you rather be?" asked Netfield. "Sitting before your fire with Nora, or out in the cemetery with Clyde?"

"That kind of talk won't get you anywhere, Mr. Netfield," said McDonald. "Nora said you'd do that, try to scare us."

"You'll help me best by leaving me alone," said Netfield. "Will you? Do I have your word on it?"

McDonald nodded reluctantly.

Netfield smiled, suddenly, warmly. "And that goes for Nora too."

Netfield took off his hat, whipped it absently against

his thigh, and put it back on his head. As he turned to leave, McDonald said, "Did you see the man?"

"What man?" asked Netfield.

"The man that was in here asking for you about an hour ago. Some stranger. An old-like kind of man and pretty dirty. I didn't care too much for him. He says you can find him at the Lucky Shoe Blacksmith Shop. I wouldn't bother, if I was you."

Netfield asked, "Was he a puncher?"

"No," said McDonald. "He said he was a wolfer."

Netfield hesitated, interested. Wolfers were wanderers. Moving from range to range, they hired themselves to ranchers, or combines of ranchers, as professional exterminators of wolves. There was no reason in the world for any wolfer whatever to be inquiring for George Netfield.

"Did he give his name?" asked Netfield.

"Yes. Rawlins. Mr. Morgan Rawlins, of Deer Lodge, Montana."

Wingate said, "I knew a Rawlins back in Tennessee."

"But you didn't know a man named Morgan Rawlins, of Deer Lodge Montana," said Netfield. "There's a federal penitentiary at Morgan, Colorado. There's a penitentiary at Rawlins, Wyoming. And the Montana pen, of course, is at Deer Lodge. Here's a man with a remarkable sense of humor. He names himself for three calabooses. Maybe I'd better see what this is all about."

Smiling faintly, he left the Blue Banner.

The Lucky Shoe Blacksmith Shop was across the railroad tracks, at the dead end of an alley. It was a great shed with double doors. The doors were now open, and deep in its interior the smith worked at his forge. On the hard earth to one side of the shop, shabby in the sun, stood a ramshackle two-wheeled wolfer's cart with two spavined-looking mares. As Netfield walked up, there were but two people in sight, the smith within at his work, and a second man sitting on his heels in the thin shade of the cart.

This man, Netfield judged, was about sixty-two years old and wore tin-rimmed spectacles. He was ragged, puny, collapsed-looking, and wore two guns. His clothes were foul with sweat and grime.

Netfield came to a stop, and said, "Mr. Rawlins?"

The old-timer looked at him with mucous-red eyes. "If you say so."

"The wolfer?"

"If you say so."

"I never saw a two-gun wolfer before," said Netfield politely.

"That's the way it goes," said the old-timer. "Something new every day. You George Netfield?"

Netfield nodded.

"Bucky Smith sent me. He said you wanted to hire a gunhand."

"Well, I don't," said Netfield. "It was all a mistake. What's your real name?"

"My real name is the Turtle Creek Kid. I better tell you right now I ain't so much as a gunfighter any more, what with my spectacles and rheumatism and all, but I don't find your looks too hard to take so I accept the job. Besides, this can't be much of a job anyways."

"You don't understand," said Netfield gently. "I don't need you. I don't want you."

"Don't keep saying that," said the Kid crossly. "And I better tell you right now I'm mercenary. I come high. I'm going to cost you two hunnert dollars a month."

"Not me," said Netfield. "Because I don't hire gunhands."

"In advance," said the Kid.

Netfield laughed. "You've been to trouble and expense getting here. You've got it coming to you. Stop around at the Blue Banner about suppertime and pick it up."

"I'll do that," said the Kid. "Satisfaction guaranteed. Bucky told me what the deal is. Bend over."

Netfield bent over. The Kid made a funnel of his dirt-encrusted hands, put them to Netfield's ear, and in a fetid breath whispered, "You're lucky to git me."

The old-timer got stiffly to his feet. He stepped back a few yards, studied Netfield for a moment, then said, "I always like to know just where I stand. I see you're wearing a gun. Get it out of its holster."

Netfield made his draw, and replaced his weapon.

He had always had gun-talent close to wizardry, but never demonstrated it. He demonstrated it now; his Colt came out of its leather like the flick of a mirror and vanished.

The Turtle Creek Kid looked disgusted.

"Oh, well," he said. "That's what I git for being a ole broke-down invalid. I gotta nursemaid little children."

But as Netfield made his way to the Jerome House, his mind was not on the Turtle Creek Kid. He liked the fumbling, grimy old man, but dismissed him from his consciousness almost as soon as he separated from him.

He brooded as he walked, and knew he loved this sleepy little town, the town which he had helped to build. He felt a deep attachment to its quiet, respectable citizenry, decent hardworking folk about to be dominated and strangled by a lawlessness beyond their comprehension.

Suddenly he realized he had an obligation to these people equal to, even greater than, his obligation to himself.

And with this came a bleak decision. He must move into the offensive himself . . . ruthlessly, intelligently, and instantly.

The foremost urgency, of course, was to prove to Cimarron the urgency of the situation.

He had tried this, and failed. He must try it again, first laying irrefutable groundwork.

Faynopolis must certainly hold the proof he needed. This must have all started in Faynopolis, beyond the southern mountains.

He decided he must make a trip to Faynopolis.

Too, Spunky Martin was at Faynopolis, and Netfield had unfinished business with Spunky.

Just short of the Jerome House, Netfield passed Efferson's store. A clerk was standing just within the doorway, arranging a display of plush caps. When he saw Netfield, he said, "Andy wants to talk to you, Mr. Netfield. He just stepped over to Miss Cimarron's house but he'll be back before too long."

"I'll drop around and see him there," said Netfield. "Thanks."

The harsh afternoon sun pumiced the great Crewe house as Netfield came up the walk. He bypassed the front, with its ornate two-storied verandas, and took the little patch along the east side of the building; here, about two thirds of the way to the rear, was a small door. This, he knew, was the door to the late Colonel Crewe's office, the door for his business visitors, the true door to vast Crewe enterprises. Netfield chose this door at this time so that Cimarron might feel that this was not a social visit.

He knocked, and Andy Efferson admitted him.

"They said you wanted to see me," said Netfield.

"I do," said Efferson. "Come in. I'll tell you about it a little later."

Netfield stepped inside. He followed Efferson down a short hall, into the office.

The luxury of the small office astounded Netfield. Its subdued elegance was something he might have expected ot see in a St. Louis bank, perhaps, but not in Kirkville. Its walls were of black walnut paneling, softly waxed, and the carpet on its floor was a rich emerald green. Its one window, looking out onto the stables at the rear, was narrow and tall and hung with green velvet draperies, caught back with golden cords and tassels. There was no sign of a safe, filing cabinets, or ledgers. The furniture consisted of several comfortable lounge chairs, and the table. This table, in the center of the room, was the natural center of interest. It was of teak, not large but massive, and had its own chair of massive teak; both table and chair were deeply carved. It wasn't a throne, but, Netfield thought, it was certainly the next thing to one. Cimarron sat in the teak chair, behind the teak table, and watched them enter. She smiled graciously, but impersonally.

Netfield said, "This was Mr. Efferson's idea. I came to see him, not you."

"If you'll excuse my speaking bluntly," said Cimarron.

"If you'll excuse *my* speaking bluntly," said Netfield.

"But now that you're here," said Cimarron, "you feel it your duty to repeat—"

"I have nothing to repeat," said Netfield. "And nothing whatever to discuss with you. Not at the moment."

They smiled at each other, stiffly but pleasantly.

Elton Colfax came into the room. They heard him first coming down the hall, from the direction of the house proper, not from the side door, and then he was standing among them.

When he saw Netfield, he simply shook his head, in belittling scorn, and showed no particular anger. This was the worst of all possible signs to Netfield, for it indicated that Colfax knew himself to be safely entrenched. He looked as though he had been traveling.

Netfield said pleasantly, "Don't tell me you live here now, Mr. Colfax?"

"No," said Colfax shortly.

"Then how did you get in?"

"I got in through the front door."

Netfield said, "We didn't hear you break it down."

"It was unlocked," said Colfax, as though he were talking to an idiot child. "It was unlocked, so I just walked in."

Netfield turned to Cimarron. "You just heard the man express his life philosophy, I'm afraid. When he finds an unlocked door, he walks in."

"And what's wrong with that?" asked Colfax, frowning.

Colfax's manner was completely unruffled, and his very

tranquillity gave Netfield a chill. It told him that the Dunphy crowd considered the situation completely in hand. That they were riding even higher than Netfield suspected. As Netfield studied Colfax, Colfax studied the room. Not studying it as though it were new to him, but studying it with an interested inventory-look.

He stood in the center of the room, a blocky giant with a Greek god profile going slightly to dewlaps. He was a vain man, and now he wore expensive come-to-town clothes. His eyes swept the room and came magnetically, obliquely, to the desk and chair occupied by Cimarron. Not to Cimarron, but to that authoritative desk and chair.

He was standing in such a position that the window to the backyard was before him, and behind Cimarron. After a bit, he turned his head and stared out the window; Netfield followed the direction of his gaze.

Netfield could see a segment of the yard, and the stable. A beautiful golden mare, Cimarron's favorite mount at C Bar C, Hyacinth, stood tied to an iron ring by the stable door.

Colfax said, "Miss Cimarron, I just came in from C Bar C. I don't know whether I did right or not, but I came in on Hyacinth."

He walked to the window and stared into the yard.

Cimarron looked annoyed, but when she spoke her voice was steady and courteous. "Why, of course, Elton," she said. "That's quite all right."

"She strained a tendon, or something," Colfax said. "But now she seems to be standing okay. I guess she's over it."

Cimarron arose and came to the window beside him.

Casually, Colfax turned. He sauntered to the desk and dropped into the massive chair behind it.

Netfield looked at Efferson, Efferson at Netfield, and each at Cimarron. She seemed unaware of what had really happened.

It had come upon Colfax like a craving to sit in that authoritative chair, Netfield knew, and he had been unable to resist resorting to craft to attain it. Now, he looked pompous, kingly, and arrogant.

Now, too, he addressed Netfield.

"Where you from, Netfield?" he asked.

"A place called Baxter Springs," said Netfield amiably.

"Ever get homesick?" asked Colfax.

"No," said Netfield.

"I can't understand these fellows that do all this long-distance roving," smirked Colfax. "A lot of them dies far from home, gets buried, and gets forgotten."

"That's true," said Netfield. "Gloomy, but true."

He turned to Efferson. "Shall we go, Andy?"

Efferson, Cimarron, and Netfield left the room, walked down the hall, and stood for a moment in the sunlight by the sidedoor.

Cimarron said, "I know as well as you, Mr. Netfield, what happened in there. But I understand, and you don't. Elton is just a big boy at heart. My father used to sit in that chair, and it has a fascination for Elton. It has a great importance in his mind. He wanted to sit in it, so he told me that made-up story about Hyacinth and sat in it."

"We'll start at the beginning," said Netfield. "What's he doing riding Hyacinth in the first place?"

She flushed, but said nothing.

"And about the desk and chair," said Netfield, "who are we to say whether he sits in it or not?"

She turned an angry red. "What do you mean we? It's my chair, isn't it?"

"No," said Netfield mildly. "You just think it's your chair. Actually, it's Web Dunphy's."

"That'll be enough of that, George," said Efferson. "Come along."

They left her on the doorstep, taut, furious, and shaken.

Halfway back to Main Street, Efferson said, "Here's what I wanted to tell you, George. I saw an old man on the street today that I remember from my Texas days. He's old and shabby and decrepit now, but he was poison when he was at his peak. They called him the Turtle Creek Kid around Mobeeti, and they claimed he was unbeatable with the six-gun. In those days he was a professional killer, and no one knew his tally."

"Maybe he came to Kirkville for a rest," said Netfield. "If he's all that old and useless, maybe he came to settle down."

"Maybe. I just thought I'd tell you."

"Thanks," said Netfield.

XI

WHEN THE Turtle Creek Kid came to the Blue Banner that evening, he came to the back door, a frail, humble wisp of a man, half hidden by the shadows.

Netfield paid him, then in painstaking detail outlined to him the true state of affairs, up to the moment, filling in gaps left by Bucky Smith. Among other things, he inquired about Kruger, but the Kid had never heard of him, nor was he much interested in him.

"I'm going to Faynopolis," said Netfield, and outlined his plans. "I'm not sure just what I'll run into, so if you want to, you can be there to cover me. Are you known in Faynopolis?"

"No," said the Kid. "And that's why I got that wolfer's cart. A wolfer's cart can git jest about anywheres. When do you want me to start?"

"As soon as you can."

"Then git out of my way. I'll start right now."

"Fine," said Netfield, a little jolted. "I'll give you twelve hours, then follow."

As the Kid slid into the darkness, his complaining voice came in a whisper out of the night. "I want you there to cover me. I want you there to nurse me. I want you there to take keer o' me."

That evening and the night passed without event for Netfield. About seven next morning, he left the Jerome House,
had breakfast at the Mockingbird, and made his way to
the Blue Banner to post Wingate on a few minor items before his departure. The porter at the Jerome House had
taken a message to the livery barn, and his mount would
be waiting for him within a half an hour.

Wingate was in the front room of the Blue Banner, behind
the bar, shaving in the bar mirror. Netfield, after briefly
outlining once more his plans about Faynopolis, said, "Take
care of yourself, Sherrod. This business is getting bad, and
fast."

"I'm going with you," Wingate said.

Netfield simply shook his head.

McDonald, the swing man, came in sleepy-eyed, and
pulled off his coat. He was due to come in at three in the
afternoon, but for a week now, voluntarily, he had been showing up and working eighteen hours a day. Netfield and
Wingate exchanged glances of pride in him, and friendship
for him behind his back, but neither commented. McDonald
poured himself a glass of Madeira, broke a raw egg in it,
and took it at a gulp.

Wingate said, "Hangover?"

"Nora," said McDonald. "She's so worried about Mr. Netfield here that she gets me upset. I couldn't eat my fried
potatoes and sowbelly."

Wingate grinned. McDonald carried out the empty case
of beer bottles to the sidewalk, in the morning ritual of
propping open the front door.

He returned almost instantly, followed by a knot of serious
men: Sheriff Walsh, Deputy Cantrell, and Web Dunphy.

Netfield said curtly, "We're not open for business yet. Try
some place else."

Sheriff Walsh began to puff. When he spoke, his slippery
eyes looked over Netfield's right shoulder, over his left, at
his stomach, but never at Netfield's face. His hands fluttered

and fumbled through his pockets, searching, and at last came out with a paper.

He said, "Sherrod Taunton Wingate, this-here's a warrant for your arrest. I forthwith and hereby serve it."

"What's he charged with?" asked Netfield.

Dunphy and Cantrell stood quietly to one side, watching.

"You know what he's charged with," said Walsh. "He's charged with wounding two respectable citizens, Pearson Morse and Joshua M. Thayer, and bushwhacking unto death J. S. Bennett."

"Sounds like a wagon train massacre," said McDonald. "Sherrod, you been up to any wagon train massacres?"

"Not that I recall," said Wingate.

Severely, McDonald said, "If there's one thing I despise more than a criminal, it's an absent-minded criminal that can't recall his loathsome deeds. I'm ashamed of you, Sherrod."

Dunphy and Deputy Cantrell still stood silently, waiting and watching.

Netfield said, "When did this happen, Sheriff, and where?"

"You know when it happened," blustered Sheriff Walsh. "Some time back. In the lumberyard. And you were there."

"You're not referring to *that* squabble?" said Netfield, genuinely surprised.

"I sure as hell am."

"After all these days?"

"I'm a busy man. I just got around to it."

"I was there. Am I being charged too?"

"No, Mr. Netfield," said the sheriff. "You was just an innocent bystander."

"Who signed the warrant?" asked Netfield.

"Pearson Morse." The sheriff was showing signs of nervousness. "That is the feller you know as High Play."

"And Joshua Thayer must be the other. And J. S. Bennett must be the late Julian."

Gently, Netfield said, "Don't take up my time with such nonsense, Sheriff."

"I got no trouble with you, Mr. Netfield," said the sheriff. "But the law is the law, and you damn well know it. I'm serving a warrant."

"What's Web Dunphy doing here?" asked Netfield.

"I was just passing by," said Dunphy, slitting his eyes.

"Sheriff," said Netfield. "You're not going to arrest Mr. Wingate for that lumberyard business, now or ever. I mean what I say. You're a foul abomination to the badge you wear. You're a sneaking, sniveling hireling with a maggotty mouth, a disgrace to the lowest cur in the county. Get out of here!"

Dunphy said, "You're talking to the law."

"You want in on this?" asked Netfield.

"No," said Dunphy. "Not at the moment."

Netfield turned to Cantrell. "How about you?"

Cantrell's big coarse face remained masklike. He made no answer.

Placatingly, Sheriff Walsh said, "You're excited, Mr. Netfield. I won't hold it agin you. Maybe I made a mistake. I'll talk to this High Play feller agin. I'll try to get him to withdraw the charge."

"You do that," said Netfield pleasantly.

Wingate laid his finger horizontally beneath his lower lip, and spat. The scorn, the contempt in the gesture was an insult almost unbearable.

"I guess we just came in for a social visit," said Cantrell in his bullfrog voice. "Well, it was educational and I can truly say I enjoyed it."

Lazily, he added, "This is a saloon. Could it be you're open for business yet?"

Netfield nodded, and made a sign to McDonald.

McDonald set out three glasses and a bottle of whiskey.

Walsh, Dunphy, and Cantrell gathered at the bar.

Cantrell picked up two of the glasses, returned them to McDonald, and said, "I won't need these. I'm drinking alone." He poured his drink, and downed it.

Dunphy darkened at the rebuff. He left, Walsh at his heels.

Netfield said, "Mr. Cantrell, this drink is on the house."
Cantrell laid a quarter on the bartop. He said, "I pay for
my own drinks, Mr. Netfield."

He lumbered to the door, and out onto the boardwalk.

It was nine o'clock, and the sun was already crisping the
sere countryside with its heat, when Netfield left the
livery barn and rode out of town, south, toward the mountains, toward the pass and distant Faynopolis.

Before he had left, he bought a brand new Colt from
Efferson's store and put it in his holster. His regular weapon,
his favorite .45, he had wrapped in newspaper and placed
in his saddle roll.

As he traveled, he carefully bypassed all human hab-
itation. He bypassed C Bar C, Wingate's cabin with its
smokeless chimney, and, in the darkness as night came, the
precarious 7 Diamond.

He slept in the foothills.

Next morning, with the rising sun, he saw the mountains,
vaulting above him in their wild, harsh glory.

By midmorning he had found the pass, and entered it.

XII

As Netfield rode deeper into the pass, several things became apparent. First, to his surprise, he found that despite
its tangled and rock-cluttered appearance it was quite a good
trail, wide and comfortably navigable. Off from the trail,
to his left and his right, hidden or partially hidden by sand-
stone crevices and stunted cedars, were small bulblike pas-
tures, grassy and rich, ideal for holding cattle. Once, when
he stopped by a chill, sweet stream to water Beeswax and fill
his canteen, he saw cattle hoofprints in the dry clay, heading south, from Kirk County toward Faynolopis. They were
very old prints, faint from wind scourings, but there was no
doubt about it: once cattle had moved from Kirk County,
with its own fine shipping center, to distant Faynopolis and

its lesser shipping center. And that certainly sounded like stolen cattle.

There were no new cattle prints, heading north, from Bonnet County to Kirk, but these would come, for this was the plan.

The time might possibly come, according to their plan, when this innocent pass would drain off fine stolen herds from as far south as Wyoming. This was the destiny Dunphy and his friends had allotted to Kirkville.

The pass ended in a hairpin turn, and Netfield came out into Bonnet County. He passed the last of the boulders, crossed a slash of burn-over, and pressed through a thicket onto the prairie.

The air was completely without motion. Before him rolled the grass, seemingly endless, cinnamon and gray beneath the scorch of a dry summer. It was about three o'clock in the afternoon, and he took a look at the sky, his first good look for many hours.

He didn't much like what he saw.

Nine-tenths of the sky was preternaturally blue and clear, a medium-deep watery blue, the blue of a doctor's blueglass bottle, clear and entirely cloudless. On the northwestern horizon, however, there was an edging of pale gray, sluggish clouds, dirty and slightly and slightly folded, looking much like stagnant scum. The color of the deep sky here, behind and around them, was not blue but a glistening peagreen. A storm was making up here, Netfield knew, and not a swashbuckling, traveling storm, but a deadly, vicious local hell with infinite potentialities. He pressed Beeswax with the calves of his legs, and they moved southwest.

In the next four hours the lip of scum grew, accumulating slowly and so lifelessly that its growth was almost imperceptible.

At a quarter after seven, by Netfield's gold watch, he came into Faynopolis' Main Street. The air, still without a breath of motion, lay slate gray and olive on the road, and buildings, not dim but strangely bright, as though in an eerie light, reflected from water.

Faynopolis, though a county seat and Bonnet County's greatest population center, was comprised of about forty homes and shops, all of them shabby and weather-punished. South of town about a half-mile were the makeshift feeding pens and loading chutes, like silver foil in the twilight, and the tiny, inadequate railroad spur.

This was Saturday, and trading day, and on back streets spring wagons and buckboards were tied to ramshackle, paling fences. Farmers and their families were busy here, making bustling preparations to leave before 'the weather'. Along the main street things were quieter. The sidewalk was largely empty. A few cow ponies were tied before a warped, clapboard building marked STOCKMAN'S REST. At the end of the hitching rail was the Kid's team of shaggy, midget mares, their checkreins let down that they might rest, and behind them the Kid's dilapidated two-wheeled wolfer's cart.

Netfield hitched his mare and, taking a newspaper-wrapped bundle from his saddle roll, wandered up the boardwalk.

Sandwiched between a cafe and the bank was a barber-shop, brightly lighted. *Shaves, Haircuts, Macassar*, its sign said, *Razors Sharpened*. Letters at the bottom said, *Baths, 25¢ each*. He stepped inside.

There was a rancher in the barber chair, with a twisting little boy on his knees, and the barber was cutting the little boy's hair. Behind the barber, on shelves, were mugs, razor-papers, honing stone, and a featherless three-legged chicken in a fruitjar of alcohol, obviously a conversation piece.

Netfield gave the little boy a nickel, which he grabbed, and the barber twenty-five cents, and asked, "The bath?"

"What bath?" asked the barber.

Before Netfield could respond, the barber said, "Oh, you mean like it says on the sign. You mean you feel you come to the point where you have to take yourself a bath. It's been a long time since anyone's used that tub. You'll find it and a candle in the backroom, and a bucket. They's trash in the bucket and tub but just empty 'em on the floor. You'll find a pump in the alley. Should be a towel somewheres about, to. You favor soap?"

Netfield nodded and the barber, grudgingly, handed him a sliver of yellow laundry soap. Netfield walked through the door, into the backroom, found and lighted the candle.

The place was a catchall for odds and ends. By one wall was an iron cannonball stove and joints of pipe, stored for the summer. He unwrapped the newspaper. It contained his favorite .45. He examined it, rewrapped it, and put it in the stove, carefully closing the door. He next checked the Colt in his holster.

He left the barbershop, smiling noncommittally at the bewildered barber, and returned to the sidewalk.

He made his way to the Stockman's Rest, and stepped through its open door.

Inside there was no lobby—just one big room, hotel desk, diningroom, bar, and, to the rear, a short counter with a pasteboard placard reading: *Passage to any State in the Union, Bonnet County Stagelines.* Illiterately, under 'any State', someone had written, *sept to Hogtick, Texas.* There were six or eight men by the bar, cowmen and townsmen, and a few others sitting in splitbottommed chairs among the cigar butts on the floor, enjoying the homelike atmosphere. To Netfield's eye, even the mildest of the townsmen looked quietly hardcase. In a far corner, was the Kid.

In a swift, stiff stride, Netfield moved to the hotel desk. The clerk, a poker-faced young man with the hairy hands of a baboon, looked up and handed Netfield a pen.

Not touching the pen, Netfield said, "Did a letter come for me? The name is James J. Jones."

The clerk took a small batch of mail from beneath the shelf and riffled through it with the fingers of an old cardman. "No James J. Jones," he said. "I have a nice corner room upstairs, at the back—" Here he paused. "At the back, over the kitchen roof, but nice. And you'll be wanting supper, of course?"

"Now let's hold on a minute," said Netfield amiably. "I'll want that room and supper, but will you want me? I got into a little whist game at Bismark and got cleaned. I'm a cattle broker working out of Belle Fourche and my people were supposed to mail me a little emergency money. If it hasn't come, I'm not sure just what the situation is."

"I'm not sure either," said the clerk. And waited.

Netfield took out his fine gold watch. "Perhaps you could hold this for bed and food until I get a little relief."

"Perhaps I could," said the clerk.

"No," said Netfield, and returned the watch to his pocket. "I live by that timepiece."

He pushed back his coatskirt, making the motion as awkward as possible, took the spanking new Colt from its holster, and laid it on the counter.

"Eight dollars should do the trick," he said. "Will you give me eight dollars for a few days on my Colt."

"Yes," said the clerk, and reached for the weapon.

"Watch out," warned Netfield.

"I've handled loaded guns before," said the clerk, as though he were talking to a child.

"I'm not talking about its being loaded," said Netfield. "I'm talking about the oil. It's well coated with oil, and you don't want to get it all over your hands. I always keep it well oiled to preserve its value. I hate unsightly rust. There might be a little grease in the barrel too; keeps the barrel from getting pitted, you know."

By now, Netfield had an audience. Men drifted around him, listening, painfully polite.

Netfield took the eight dollars, signed the register, and returned the money to the clerk. "Hold it on account," he said laughing. "It's safer with you than it is with me."

"Yes, Mr. Jones," said the clerk.

Across the room, the Kid put on his boot, stamped it a couple of times to set it right, and walked to the desk.

With a happy grin, blinking through his spectacles, he said, "Why, howdy, Mr. Netfield. What are you doing out of Kirk County."

"My name is James J. Jones," Netfield said coldly. "I'm a cattle broker from Bismark. I've never been to Kirk County. And I never laid eyes on you before."

The Kid stepped back to get a better focus, gave Netfield a slow, intense examination, and said, "Ain't you the Netfield in Kirkville who has declared a one man war against some of the county's most decent folks? Didn't you hire a young boy named Wingate to take him a Winchester and button up the vest of a poor hardworking cowboy named Julian Richardson?"

A man yawned, scratched the back of his neck, and strolled from the room out into the night. Only as he passed the corner of Netfield's eye, did Netfield get a quick, split look at him. He wore a clean white calico shirt, collarless, with a brass collar button at the throat, and cheap, plaid woolen pants. He was bowlegged and lithe, and had the look of a cowhand turned small businessman.

To the Kid, Netfield said placatingly, "I apologize."

"For what?" said the Kid. "You didn't do nothing."

"For picking you up and arguing with you on an honest mistake. I must look like this Netfield, but I'm James J. Jones, of Fargo. That's the way it is. I hope they're no hard feelings."

"No hard feelings," said the Kid. "Hell, no. And I didn't mean to pry."

"It's been pleasant meeting you," said Netfield politely, and walked to the section of the room reserved for dining. Here were six tables in a row along the wall; he seated himself, placing his hat on the empty chair facing him, and was almost immediately attended by the clerk.

"I'll have about a two-dollar supper," said Netfield. "Mix it up according to your own judgement. And where do I wash my hands?"

"There's a washbench and basin out through the back hall,

on the back porch," said the clerk. "You'll get a big supper for two dollars."

"I want a big supper," said Netfield. He arose, crossed the room, and went down the back hall.

There was a door at the end of the hall; he opened it and walked out into the night. About him was impenetrable blackness. The air was motionless and tepid, as though imprisoned in a great bladder. He went a few doors down an alley, and, using his key, entered the barbershop storeroom. He took his .45 from the stove, and slid it in his holster. His coat tail covered it, covered everything, in fact, but the holstertip and the buckle of his gunbelt.

As he returned to the hotel, the first stray handful of rain fell in big drops, like skinned grapes in the thick dust. When it stopped, it seemed finished, exhausted.

His supper was waiting for him when he reached his table. It was quite a supper, too: ham, mutton, chicken thigh, kidney beans, potatoes and boiled onions, wheat bread and cornbread, a platter of butter brought to the table, and a huge bowl of rice and raisin pudding. He ate in silence. The Kid had vanished.

When he had finished, he nodded to the clerk behind his desk and to the room at large, and went out into the town.

Now no soul stirred on the street, and the darkness was oppressive. Suddenly, from the northwest came the first lightning, a stain of frosty green. In its incandescence, the horses at the rail sprung into vision, in detail, even to the hairs on their manes. Up and down the street a cardboard town of lavender and charcoal appeared and once more vanished. There was no sign of Spunky Martin, but Spunky, Netfield knew had received the word, and he would come.

At a leisurely pace, Netfield walked past the store fronts.

The man who appeared before him was not Spunky Martin, nor was he the yawning man whom Netfield had seen in the hotel. He stepped out from a doorway directly in Netfield's path, and Netfield saw instantly that he was a good head taller than either of these. He said, "You are unarmed, so hold steady." His voice was thick, unrecognizable with anger.

"I'm holding steady," said Netfield carefully. "Who are you?"

"Light a match," said the man, and Netfield struck a match.

In the droplet of flame, Netfield saw that he was facing Elton Colfax, dressed against the coming rain in a yellow cowboy slicker. Tight to his thigh, barrel down, he held his six-gun. His face worked in rage and, even when the match burned out, Netfield could sense that rage mounting. He's one of these upper-hand boys, Netfield thought, just give him the upper-hand, like he thinks he's got now, and he goes crazy.

Pleasantly, Netfield said, "Where's Spunky? I want to see him."

"And he wants to see you," said Colfax. "Just come along and don't make any trouble."

They walked east along the town's main street, toward the feeding yards and loading chutes. Only once did Colfax speak. Furiously, as though he had been abused, he said, "Why can't you leave other people alone? It's going to take a lot of time and a lot of hard work to patch up the damage you've caused."

"It might at that," said Netfield courteously. "And I'd like to be around when you patch up Julian."

At the edge of town there was a small building with a loading platform fronting the railroad tracks. A light showed from its rear window. It was the station, Netfield knew, and the stationmaster was back in his living quarters.

As they came abreast its door, Netfield said, "I'd like to drop in here a minute. Do I have your permission?"

"Why?"

"I feel the need of a long distance ticket."

"Why, sure," said Colfax. "That's very sensible." He seemed to be enjoying a secret joke. "You bet."

They entered the waiting room and the stationmaster came into his wicket, carrying a kitchen lamp.

"A ticket to Arizona," said Netfield. "To Yuma, Arizona."

"That sounds like a dandy place," said Colfax drolly.

Netfield laid down the money and put the ticket in his pocket. "Yes," he said.

Colfax laughed.

Again in the open, they continued east, beyond the straggling fringes of the town, along the weedgrown berm of the tracks. After a bit they came to the loading chutes and feeding pens; here they turned left and entered a shantylike building which was apparently the feeding yard office. Colfax's gun, momentarily out of sight in the station, had since been in his hand, muzzle down. Now he slipped it lazily in its holster.

XIII

THERE WERE two men in the room, sitting across the table from each other—the man in the collarless white shirt and Spunky Martin. Both were stolidly waiting. At Netfield's appearance, Spunky scrambled to his feet. His vest was off, and the 44-40 sagged in its harness under his armpit.

Ignoring Spunky and Colfax, Netfield spoke to the man in the white shirt. "Who are you? The general handyman at this one-horse thieving feeding yards?"

"Watch your tongue," the man said. "This feeding yards ain't one-horse, and it ain't thievin'. And I ain't no handyman; I own it."

"I never could stand a liar," said Netfield. "You don't own anything. My guess is that Web Dunphy from Kirkville owns it. Am I right?"

"Me and him is partners," said the man doggedly.

"Get out of here, Arnold," said Spunky Martin.

"Glad to," said the man, and left the building.

"Guess what Mr. Netfield's got," said Colfax drolly. "He stopped on the way, and bought a ticket to Arizona."

"Well, ain't that nice," said Spunky. His face was pallid with cold savagery. "A railroad ticket. Now that's a surprise."

"And I've got another surprise," said Netfield sociably. "A real one. I got a gun in my holster." His thumbs were hooked in his belt at his belly.

They stood for an instant, stupefied.

After a pause, Colfax said, "He's running a cheap bluff."

"I doubt it," said Spunky softly. He licked his upper lip. "You know what I think, Elton? I think he tricked you into coming here so he could take a crack at killing us both."

"Correct," said Netfield briskly.

"I got him for you," said Colfax. "And there he stands. He's just a saloonkeeper. You're the gunfighter."

"They's been some mighty fine gunfighters owned saloons," said Spunky. "That don't signify nothing."

"*Get to work!*" ordered Colfax.

Spunky froze and Netfield shot him. He shot him in the old professional style, as he had been taught by experts at Baxter Springs, giving himself an instant's leeway from the danger signs in Spunky's eye and jugular. Just as Spunky's gunsight cleared its leather, he stopped his first bullet. The two that followed were simply guarantees. He went to the table top, to a chair seat, and to the floor.

Colfax stood open-mouthed, paralyzed with fright and disbelief.

"I'm not a gunfighter," said Netfield quietly. "I want you to get that straight. It's just that I've always enjoyed a certain dexterity. You see the difference, don't you?"

"I'm unarmed," said Colfax. "I haven't even drawn. You're not going to shoot me down unarmed, are you?"

"Who knows?" said Netfield. "I'm a man of whim."

After a moment, he said, "Toss your gun in the corner."

Colfax obeyed, meticulously.

Netfield laid the railroad ticket on the table. "I bought this for you," he said.

Craftily, Colfax said, "I don't see how you can make me use it."

"I can't make you use it," said Netfield. "But I can sure as hell make you want to use it. You've probably heard of the old cross-the-street business. Well, I'm hanging it on you, as of now."

"Cross-the-street?" said Colfax.

"It's a little procedure that's popular in the South, and practiced, too, on occasion here in the West. Here's the way it goes. A man, say like myself, has a little trouble with a shovelful of trash, like you. I don't want to go to the trouble of horsewhipping you, or caning you. So I tell you to cross the street, and, brother, you'd better do it. When you see me walking down any walk, any time, you cross the street. If you're standing at a bar and I come in, you walk out. If you're eating at a restaurant and I enter, you get up and leave. Because you stink to my nose, and I don't want you anywhere around me."

"People will figure it out."

"They won't have to figure it out because I'll tell them. I'll explain it to anyone who happens to be standing around, and I'll explain it loud enough for you to hear."

Mumbling, Colfax said, "I couldn't take that. Not for ever."

"Of course you couldn't," said Netfield. "Eventually you'd draw on me, and that's it."

Outside, the storm broke. The wind came first in powerful little gusts, patting the creaking sides of the shanty. Then came the lightning, fulminating whitely against the window, and the clapping, ear-splitting thunder. Windblown with terrific velocity, the rain came in torrents, drenching the little building, hammering it.

"You've had your say," said Colfax slyly. "Now I'll have mine. There could be a way out of it for me."

Netfield cocked an eyebrow.

Colfax said, "I wouldn't do it, of course, but for sake of argument what about this. Say me or some friend of mine got you in the back some dark night whilst you was passing a Kirkville alley. I wouldn't never consider such a terrible thing, but you might like to stop a minute and ponder it."

"I've got an acquaintance over in the Idaho Territory," lied Netfield blandly, "and I'll tell you a little about him. He's a cowhand, crippled, fifty-two years old. He's a conscientious worker and takes pride in even the smallest job but life is closing in on him. I'm going to put it in my will that if I die a violent death, even if I get run over by a wagon, he does a trivial job and my estate pays him nine thousand six hundred dollars."

"And the trivial job is running me down, I bet, and killing me."

"He's very persistent and, as I said before, conscientious."

"You can't put a murder deal in a will. It's against public good."

"It won't be mentioned. But he and I will have agreed. The will will just say that when he goes to a certain strip of bottomland, on a day of his choice, and plows a single furrow, he collects the money. And that day will be as soon as he can get there after he fixes you up. You're not saying plowing is against public good, are you?"

His cheeks fluttering, Colfax said hoarsely, "But why that funny amount? Nine thousand six hundred."

"It's not a funny amount. I'll break it down for you. He earns forty dollars a month. Four hundred and eighty a year. Ninety-six hundred represents *wages for the next twenty years*. And no outlay. In twenty years he'll be seventy-two, with no prospects. With a few thousand now he can together a starter-herd, and fix himself for life. I can see these are figures you can understand. You don't look happy."

"That's the most wicked, devilish thing I ever heard," said Colfax.

"Yes, indeed," said Netfield.

Colfax picked up the railroad ticket.

As Netfield left the room, Colfax said numbly, "But

there's other people gunnin' for you. What if somebody else
gets you?"

Netfield said cheerfully, "We'll cross that bridge when we
come to it."

Behind his back, Colfax began to shout. "But that don't
help me none. I mean, what happens to me?"

Netfield stepped out into the pounding, slashing rain.
Head down, he started back to town.

The Turtle Creek Kid had left the Stockman's Rest, and
after a little searching Netfield located him in an alley
cabin, in a smoky horse-traders' doggery known as the
Musselshell Cafe. He was seated alone at a table in a corner, on a nailkeg with a drumhead seat of rawhide. He was
drinking forty-rod from a cutdown tin can; many old-
timers held you had to taste tin to really taste whiskey. When
Netfield came up and stood over him, he said, "Why, I do
believe you been out in that rain."

"Spunky Martin's dead," Netfield said. "Colfax is high-
tailing for Arizona. And Web Dunphy owns the feeding
yards here. We're really pushing them and from here on
things are going to explode. If you want to get out, now's
the time."

The Turtle Creek Kid grinned. "I don't want to get out."

"Then where were you tonight when you were needed?"

"How was I needed?"

"To hold an umbrella for me," said Netfield.

"Now you're being sourcastic," said the Kid. "You're here,
ain't you? Mean and mad and alive? I declare to mercy I
don't know what's got your dander up. Maybe you'd like
a drink?"

"No."

"Well, there's something wrong. Maybe you're hungry.
This place specializes in fine old-fashioned Southern cooking.
Maybe you'd like a bowl of turnipgreens and boiled chit-
lings. I'll have to leave the table when they're served, o'
course, because, as you know, chit'lings is slimy little pig-

gut and the very sight of them turns my stummick, but some folks loves 'em."

"I'm starting back to Kirkville," Netfield said. "Now."

The Kid looked shocked. "In all this wet rain?"

"The rain's about over. Well, when will I see you?"

"I don't scarcely know. I ain't a freight car and I loathe and despise traveling on a schedule. But I'll be there."

As Netfield turned to leave, the Kid said quietly and with affection, "You know something, George? You're a pretty good man with a gun. An edge better than me when I was your age."

Netfield stood stockstill.

"But not better'n me now," said the Kid placidly. "So don't go puffing out your wattles."

Netfield was about three miles out of Faynopolis when the rain changed from steel needles to gentle spray, and stopped. He pushed Beeswax steadily, not to the pass, for he thought it not unlikely that Bonnet County had its own version of Sheriff Walsh, possibly even now assembling a skeleton posse. Coming at last to a pocket in the mountains, he slept and rested his splendid bay.

A little after dawn, he came to a tiny trappers' store in the crotch of two raw claybanks, buried in a haze of scrub and greasewood. Here he laid in supplies. He bought soda crackers, cheese, canned salmon, and an onion, and put them in his saddlebag.

Beeswax, grainfed, was in fine fettle.

The morning was already blistering hot when he headed due north, toward the mountains.

XIV

THE SUN was westering when, following an abandoned trail, he crossed the last mountain spine annd came out onto a timbered ledge. Below him, stretching northward, lay Kirk

County. Beneath him, almost directly beneath him, lay 7 Diamond. He sat his saddle a moment among the pines, studying it from his lofty, hidden perch. It was truly a scrubby outfit. It was comprised of the customary clutter of buildings and outbuildings, but its ranch house was simply an oversized shed, in slovenly neglect. Tucked secretively into the foothills, it looked exactly as it was, sinister. Beyond it Netfield knew, over the rolling grass lay C Bar C, and beyond C Bar C, Kirkville. He turned in his saddle, creaking the leather a little, and examined his surroundings.

Beneath him, too, but slightly to his right, he could see the upper end of the passmouth. Between him and the pass-mouth, lay a tumbledown cabin. For a good five minutes, he inspected this cabin.

This, Netfield knew, was the cabin of Big Quinty, brother of Quinty the road-ranch keeper. Big Quinty's reputation was equally bad as that of his brother. Netfield knew him for a petty, scabby trader who bought furniture and travelworm cattle from destitute emigrants and charged cruel prices, which were little better than robbery. Like his brother, Big Quinty was known as an outlaw sympathizer.

To the east of the Quinty cabin, feeding down-slope into Kirk Valley, lay Two Feather River, with its headwaters and breaks, now concealed from Netfield by ridges and timber.

Touching Beeswax on the shoulder, Netfield turned her to his right, and walked her down the mountainside toward the Quinty cabin.

He came upon the cabin from the rear and as he circled it to the front he came suddenly upon Big Quinty. Big Quinty, like his brother, garbed himself in filthy deerhide. He was a soggy mass of a man, with milky eyes and a drooping underlip. As Netfield surprised him, he stood on his log doorstep staring intently at the empty passmouth.

Big Quinty, Netfield knew, would be well informed on any event of importance that might have transpired in the county during Netfield's absence. By causual and devious questioning, Netfield hoped to learn what, if anything, might have happened. He was organizing his line of questioning, when he happened to notice Big Quinty's expression.

To his amazement, Big Quinty appeared to be grief-stricken.

"Mr. Netfield," said Big Quinty. "Am I glad to see you! Oh, am I glad to see you!"

Netfield brought his mare to a cautious halt, and waited. As Big Quinty seemed momentarily to have lost the power of speech, Netfield asked tersely, "Why?"

"It's Rosella," said Big Quinty.

Rosella, Netfield knew, was his little four-year-old daughter.

"And what's Rosella been up to?" asked Netfield.

"She ain't been up to nothing," Quinty said. "I'm trying to tell you she's sick."

"I'm sorry," said Netfield quickly. "Very sick?"

"Unto death," said Quinty. "When it first took her, I thought it was nothing. Now I think it's that diptheria. She's rolling and tossing on her bed, out of her head, and pumping her throat like a fish, trying to breathe. I got to get a doctor to her, still I'm scared to leave her. Can that big bay you're ridin' make any time?"

Netfield nodded.

"Then get into Kirkville," said Quinty. "And get help. And take the shortest route."

The two men stared at each other.

Netfield said, "The shortest route is through 7 Diamond. You know as well as I do that 7 Diamond has a bounty on me."

Quinty began to plead. "You'll git through. You're on a errand o' mercy."

After a moment of indecision, Netfield nodded.

He started Beeswax down the trail. After a few yards, the trail bent. Now, for an instant, the front of the cabin and Big Quinty vanished from his view. The back of the cabin came into view, with its henhouse and scraggy garden. A little girl, little Rosella in the flesh, appeared in the kitchen doorway. She waved at Netfield joyously, tripped out into the backyard, and began playing with a pet goat.

Well, thought Netfield, *so that's Big Quinty's game. He was watching the passmouth, expecting me. Primed with his little trick to steer me deliberately onto 7 Diamond land.*

The word has gone round, and a trap was set for me.

Without hesitation, he turned his bay from the path and headed toward the Breaks. This was the longest, roughest, but safest route home.

It was an hour and a half later before he came into the Breaks themselves.

The Two Feather Breaks were a rocky, brushy hell of jumbled miniature valleys and spurs, pockmarked and shattered cliffs, and snarled, fingerlike canyons. It was country completely strange to Netfield, but he had heard much about it. The best route through, he had been told, was an ancient Cheyenne and old buffalo-hunting trail. It was by locating this trail and following it that he entered this stark, terrible fairyland.

At times great walls of rock, scarcely stirrup-width apart, rose damply above him, and the trail was gray and sunless before him; at times, in the open, the setting sun burned murky red on basins of littered, bone-dry leafrock. By the lifting of her tail, Beeswax showed her first faint signs of weariness.

He had just passed through such a slotlike canyon, and had come into such an open space, when the sun set. Before him was a stony amphitheater, sloping gently downward. Behind him was the last ragged line of broken cliffs. With the setting of the sun, a fabulously beautiful color change took place before his eyes, and, unconsciously, he reined his mare to a halt to observe. One instant the rocky rubble about him glowed like ruby; the next, it changed to deep gold and, as the first forerunners of twilgiht came up from the nooks and crevices, pooled into mauve and green and dove gray. It was this moment of waiting and observing that saved his life.

Someone among his ambushers, giving under the strain, fired prematurely.

Swinging his mare behind a loaf-shaped slab of granite, he dropped to the earth and slid his Winchester from its boot.

With that single loud rifle crack, he understood the whole thing instantly. Big Quinty had lured him into a trap, all right, and this was the trap. First he had told Netfield his lie and pretended to steer Netfield through 7 Diamond. Then he had staged little Rosella's appearance to divert him. Cunningly, Big Quinty had pulled the old double bluff. The ambush had been set up here in the Breaks, and it had been Quinty's duty to deliver Netfield into its hands.

Now Netfield took his bearings. To the left of the slab of granite, heaped against it, was a mound of three-foot, biscuit-shaped boulders. Spread-eagled to the earth behind his barricade, he studied the terrain through an aperture.

Before him lay the rock-cluttered amphitheater. There was no one in sight.

For perhaps ten minutes, he watched. There was no movement, nor further sound.

Abruptly, a voice called out in front of him. To his amazement, he realized it was the voice of Sheriff Walsh. "Give yourself up, Mr. Netfield. I'm placing you under arrest."

"Good evening, Sheriff," called Netfield. "What is this all about?"

"I'm placing you under arrest for killing a man down in Faynopolis."

Already, they knew. Web Dunphy's grapevine was efficient.

When Netfield made no response, Walsh called, "I wouldn't give no trouble. I brought a posse with me."

"I don't see them," answered Netfield.

Directly before him, perhaps sixty yards away, Deputy Cantrell revealed himself for an instant from behind a rocky shelter. Revealed himself, and disappeared.

"That's no posse," retorted Netfield. "Or is it?"

"I got more," yelled Walsh. "Show yourselves, boys. But be careful."

One by one, they rose up, four of them, from their scattered hiding places. Four 7 Diamond hands.

"No business, I'm afraid," declared Netfield amiably. "You might as well go home. I don't like your friends."

Even as he spoke, Netfield wondered. For one thing, Walsh was a thorough coward, yet his voice showed no fear, nothing but self-satisfaction. Reasoning told Netfield that things were not exactly as they seemed. Now, for the first time, he studied the terrain behind him, and to either side.

Dusk was fast thickening. Perception at the moment was still clear, but there was no color save for the lavender gray of the granite and the soft charcoal of the shadows. Uneasiness grew in Netfield, and he glued his gaze on his mare's ears. They were tilted forward.

Like the needle on a compass, they pointed to a pair of boulders to Netfield's right, and rear, about twenty feet away.

Sheriff Walsh called, "This is legal. I'll read you the warrant." He began a singsong recitation.

He has good eyes, if he can read in this twilight, thought Netfield grimly, and concentrated his attention on the twin boulders. Between them was a narrow crevice, spongy black with shadow.

A man emerged in a spiderlike crouch, a gun in each hand, and Netfield shot him.

The man spun, half rose, and dropped, almost at Netfield's thigh.

Netfield bent over him. It was High Play, of 7 Diamond, Mr. Pearson Morse, according to the conversation in the Blue Banner. Netfield took off the dead man's boots.

With the crash of Netfield's rifle shot, Sheriff Walsh's voice sliced off into silence.

Netfield grasped the boots by their tops. In a sweeping throw, he tossed them into the open. They lay like two black cats, motionless on the slate-gray earth.

After a pause, Sheriff Walsh asked, "What's them?"

"Boots," said Netfield. "Just an old pair of boots."

He could almost feel the wave of shock from the men that faced him.

Then, like a lunatic hell, came the rifle shots. The air seemed filled with flaking stone and burnt powder and screaming ricochets. Netfield hugged the earth, and waited. The frenzied fusillade seemed endless. After a moment, however, it dwindled, then stopped.

Now Cantrell arose from behind his rock and started in a bullish zigzag run across the clearing, heading toward Netfield. The dusk was too thick for gunsight, but Netfield aligned him down his Winchester barrel. Aligned him, but instinctively waited.

As Cantrell ran, a great shout came out of his stupid-looking face.

He bellowed, "To hell with all of you!"

Now 7 Diamond rifles opened on him. He wove, stumbled, and plowed forward, wading through the crossfire. He collapsed behind the barricade, breathing like a panting animal, close to Netfield's side.

"Did they get you?" asked Netfield quietly.

"Who cares?" said Cantrell savagely.

"What's this all about?" asked Netfield. "Why are you here?"

"How should I know?" said Cantrell. "A funny kind of righteousness come into me. I took all I can from them fellers. I'm a cattleman, not a low-down thief and bush-whacker."

After a moment, Netfield said, "You'll do. But I have a feeling they're going to kill both of us."

"Then, by golly, I'll die happy," said Cantrell in his bull-frog voice.

Sheriff Walsh's voice, a little tremulous now, came through the gloom. "Bert, you gone crazy?"

"I sure have," yelled Cantrell. "And you ought to try it yourself. It's wonderful."

Complete, utter silence fell across the clearing.

The ambush had turned into a battle, and the battle into a deadlock.

Behind their rocks, Netfield knew, the 7 Diamond men must be reappraising things.

When Sheriff Walsh next spoke, there was a conciliatory note in his voice. "I'm coming out alone," he called. "I want to talk to you Mr. Netfield."

That would be Sheriff Walsh, Netfield thought grimly, always an opportunist, always ready to adjust a situation to his profit. Now he had in mind some sort of temporary compromise.

Netfield made no answer.

The sheriff moved out into the open and walked with pompous reserve toward the center of the clearing.

"Come no farther!" warned Netfield.

The sheriff moved his hands (Netfield later realized in a peace sign) and Netfield shot him. Overlapping Netfield's shot, came a savage volley from 7 Diamond, jerking and hammering his body to the ground. Netfield, turning to Cantrell, saw the deputy had also joined the slaughter. His rifle stock was at his shoulder; he was levering in a new shell, and there was an expression of beatific joy on his face.

"You shot him deliberately, uselessly," said Netfield sternly.

"Well, let's say I joined in," said Cantrell. Suddenly, he looked not quite so oafish. "He had it in his mind to come here and talk to us. Nothing good ever come out of that man's talk. I've had my share of it, and I know."

In the lull that followed, Cantrell said speculatively, "Well, I do believe this makes me the new sheriff. I'll tell you what. Let's you and me get back a little of our own. Let's you and me spread out and put them 7 Diamond fellows under arrest, and I mean right now. I'm the sheriff, and who says I can't arrest my own posse if I want to?"

"Maybe that better wait," said Netfield, his face running sweat. "Maybe we'd better get out of here."

But already 7 Diamond was withdrawing. Even as Netfield spoke, they heard the clatter of horses hooves exploding into a demoralized retreat, diminishing into the distance. The odds had been too critically changed. This darkening pocket of rock held nothing for them now but equal risk.

After a bit, Cantrell disappeared and returned with his mount. Single file, he and Netfield wove their way down the old buffalo trail. The moon was high in a tranquil sky when they left the last of the shadowed fangs of the Breaks, and came out onto the rolling lake of grass.

Cramped and fatigued, they reached Kirkville at dawn. They parted wordlessly on the empty street, stolidly but for a single incident. Netfield offered Cantrell a crooked stogie, took one for himself, and Cantrell lighted them with a sulphurous lucifer. In the little bloom of blue-white light, the men smiled at each other—small, tight smiles, more of the eyes than of the lips. They were smiles of friendship and quiet esteem.

XV

IN HIS ROOM at the Jerome House, Netfield slept until noon. Waking, he bathed and shaved, making it almost a hedonistic rite, and went down onto the street in his best broadcloth and linen. Stiff from the saddle, and not too hungry, he had a meager meal at the Mockingbird. He was on his way to the Blue Banner when Cimarron stepped out of a millinery and mantuamaker's shop and intercepted him. She seemed preternaturally serious. Her light C Bar C buckboard was at the rail. "I'd like to talk to you," she said. "Can I have a minute of your time?"

"That depends," said Netfield.

"On what?" she asked.

"On where we talk, and what we talk about."

"I want to talk to you about a lot of things. We can take a drive in the buckboard, out of town, where we won't be overheard."

"No," said Netfield. "Talk right here."

Her upper lip went white in anger.

After a moment, she said, "Very well. Main Street is alive with a dozen garbled stories of what happened last evening at the Breaks. Mr. Cantrell, he's our new sheriff now, promoted by the County Commission, says you and he and Walsh were bushwhacked by a band of roving outlaws. What really happened?"

"I was so busy I didn't notice."

She held out her hand, spread her fingers, and examined them absently. In a very low voice, she said, "There's a horrible tension in town. Most people can't sense it, but I can. I'm beginning to agree with you. I think things are very bad."

"I've changed my mind," said Netfield. "I don't think things are bad. I think they're wonderful."

"They say, too, that you were down in Faynopolis and had some kind of trouble."

"I was *in* some trouble," said Netfield cheerfully. "But I didn't *have* any, not myself. I shot Spunky Martin, bought Elton Colfax a ticket to Yuma, and proved to my absolute satisfaction that Web Dunphy is planning on large-scale cattle running."

It put her almost in a coma. When she spoke, she said, "I don't believe it, any of it."

"Anything else?" asked Netfield politely.

"Yes," she said. "A second ago, when I asked you to ride with me in the buckboard, you refused. Was it personal?"

"It was indeed," said Netfield.

She flinched. "You mean you find my companionship unpleasant?"

"Not unpleasant," said Netfield reasonably. "Just risky."

"In what way?"

"Say I'd get in your buckboard. And you'd drive me out to some canyon. And someone, Web Dunphy or someone, would rise up from the brush and shoot me in the back. That would be pretty stupid of me, wouldn't it?"

Concealing his amusement, he observed the impact of

his words. Her soft eyelashes flew up, her back arched stiffly, and her mouth squared itself in shock.

Outraged, she said, "You think I'd do a thing like that to you?"

Woodenly, gravely, he said, "Why not? You work for Web Dunphy just like all the rest, don't you?"

Taking a snowy handkerchief from his pocket, he wiped his wrists. Conversationally, as he turned to leave, he said, "Today's going to be another scorcher."

Behind his back, as he walked away, he heard her say, "You come back here. George Netfield, you come back here."

He paid no attention.

Miss Ernestine's handy man was sitting on a bench on the boardwalk, before the Star Gunsmith Shop. He was a humped little man in hand-me-down overalls and patched boots, and was one of Netfield's oldest and closest friends. He was known simply as George, and was pitiful to behold. Only Miss Ernestine and Netfield knew that he owned a small but profitable goldmine down South. He considered himself retired and worked for Miss Ernestine because he liked her, and because he enjoyed the lively atmosphere of a parlor-house. As Netfield approached, he said, "Howdy, George," and Netfield said, "Howdy to you, George."

"Well," drawled the handy man. "They've went out with their shovels."

"Who went where?" asked Netfield.

"Some of them upstanding 7 Diamond fellers, to the Breaks, to bury honest Sheriff Walsh."

And to bury High Play, Netfield thought.

"How come you and Cantrell didn't bury him?" asked the handy man.

"It was so dark we couldn't find him," said Netfield, and added as an afterthought, "Besides we were in a hurry."

"Now that's reasonable," said the handy man with a twinkle. "Excuse me for askin'."

When he next spoke, he scarcely moved his lips. He said, "Miss Ernestine wants to see you."

"When?" asked Netfield.

"Now," said the handy man, and Netfield swung away from him, up Main Street.

He started south across Main, and had just reached the railroad tracks in the middle of the street, when he heard his name called jovially, and halted and turned. Web Dunphy was standing before the Antlers, engaged in small talk with a knot of ranchers and townsmen; he left the group, strode out into the street, and joined Netfield. He seemed somehow comfortably contented.

Allowing a touch of revulsion to wash across his face, Netfield paused in annoyance.

"Been pretty busy, Mr. Netfield?" Dunphy asked.

"Yes," said Netfield. "And I'm going to be busier."

"That could well be true,". said Dunphy.

He cleared his throat and, casually, conversationally, he said, "I ever tell you about that yellow catfish we had when I was a boy back in Missouri?"

"Some other time," said Netfield.

"Now," said Dunphy. "Well, my father had this big yellow cat he caught in the creek. We had some brined beef that was spoiling in the barrel and we had to eat it fast, not to lose it. So the catfish had to wait. Back of the house, in a crotch of the hills, was a big spring. My father put the cat in this spring. All day long the cat would swim around and around the edge of the spring. We used to laugh at him. He was doing a heap of traveling, and he thought he was getting somewhere."

"But he wasn't," said Netfield.

"That's the idea. He wasn't. When the time come to eat him, we just ditched the spring, and drained it, and cut his throat."

"And you think I'm like that yellow catfish," said Netfield.

"You're the one that put it in words, not me."

"I'm in something of a hurry," said Netfield, "but now that we're reminiscing, I'll make a small contribution. When I was a child in Baxter Springs, there was a feebleminded renegade named Windy Jones who used to come into town from the Indian Territory, throwing his weight around, scaring the wits out of decent, harmless people with his loud, vicious bluster. One day he tried to take a new fowling piece away from a greenhorn teacher, and the teacher just snapped the double triggers and shot him. But that's not the point of the story. The point of the story is the funeral. Folks came from three counties."

Cautiously, Dunphy asked, "Why?"

"They gave Windy Jones a double funeral. They buried him in two sections. In a coffin, and in a cigarbox."

Despite himself, Dunphy asked, "What did they put in the cigarbox?"

"Why, they put Windy in the cigarbox, and he fitted it fine."

"What did they put into the coffin?"

"His dear departed bluster," said Netfield, turning to leave.

Walking in slow, solemn dignity, he passed the loading platform of the station, crossed the tracks, and the south half of the roadway, and came up on the sidewalk by the lumberyard. Continuing south, he traversed the area of tumble-down shanties and weeds, and came to South Congress Street, Piano Street.

When he reached Miss Ernestine's, with its enormous hitching rail, he moved up the housewalk to the narrow porch, stood beneath the canopy of tangled honeysuckle vines, and rapped on the door panel. One of the girls—Maizie, he thought—let him in, pointed past the newelpost up steep hallway stairs, and said, "Last room at the end of the hall, on your left. She's waiting for you."

Netfield mounted the steps, went down the hall, and spoke

his name before a paint-blistered door. "Come in," called Miss Ernestine, and he entered.

The bedroom-sitting room was small and orderly, scrupulously clean, and modest in its appointments. There was a small iron bed, white enamelled, with a lyre back, a washstand with pitcher and bowl, two pine chairs and a table. Miss Ernestine sat at the table, bulbous in her black tafetta, her jowls dusted with rice powder. Her glazed, predatory eyes were glued on a little maroon book, gold stamped with the title: *Little Mistress Pamela Comes of Age: A Lexicon of Etiquette for the Young Debutante*. Miss Ernestine devoured books on etiquette and the art of social graces as avidly as a schoolboy devoured penny-dreadfuls. And for precisely the same reason; to be transported into an unbelievable, glittering dreamworld. She was a compendium of information on fashion's most obscure formalities, and her hunger could never be satisfied.

"George," she said, over her shoulder. "Did you know when you send in your calling card from the carriage, you turn down the upper lefthand corner when you want to say—"

"In Baxter Springs," said Netfield gravely, "if you got caught turning down the corner of a card, you were in trouble."

"I'm talking about calling cards, not playing cards," said Miss Ernestine petulantly, "and you mighty well know it. Why aren't you out with your 7 Diamond friends attending to Good Sheriff Walsh?"

Staring at her kindly, Netfield said, "Did you summon me here to fuss at me?"

"No," said Miss Ernestine placidly. "But I do enjoy it." After a moment, she said, "What's this I hear about you and Cimarron Crewe?"

"Nothing," said Netfield.

"You could do worse," said Miss Ernestine severely. Entirely without guile, she added, "I would be proud to have that child as a daughter."

Netfield met her eyes squarely, and made no comment.

"George," she said at length, "Kruger's back in town."

In the slice of silence that followed, there was only the ticking of the banjo clock on the wall and the faintest of rustling from Miss Ernestein's black tafetta dress.

"Maizie, coming home last night about two o'clock, saw him going into the Antlers," Miss Ernestine said.

"Thank you," said Netfield.

"Maybe he's just passing through," said Miss Ernestine.

"No, this is it—the big business."

"Locate him, and move first," advised Miss Ernestine.

"That's easier said than done," said Netfield. "You can be sure he's well hidden. He could be at the Antlers, in a loft at the feeding yards, almost any place. We'll see him when he's ready, and not before."

As Netfield reached for the china doorknob to leave, Miss Ernestine said, "When you're an old woman like me, and have seen as many gun artists as I have, you kind of get a sixth sense about them. It could well be that Mr. Kruger is the worst that Kirkville has ever seen, or ever will see."

"If you say so, it's good enough for me," said Netfield quietly, and left.

As Netfield came in sight of Main Street, he saw that the 2:17, westbound, was just pulling from the station. He was halfway across the street, when he heard the commotion. He was scarcely a dozen feet away, when he paused to take it in.

Five roistering cowboys, pretending to be drunk, were on the loading platform, smashing up a buggy. They were aware of Netfield's presence but ignored him. Three of them he recognized at 7 Diamond men; the other two he knew well as C Bar C hands.

The buggy was an especially fancy specimen, a splendor of yellow ash, glistening black patent leather, and brass lamps with big red glass bulls'-eyes. It had the factory look about it, and had apparently just been unloaded from the 2:17.

The punchers were destroying it systematically, battering and smashing it with two-by-fours and the stationmaster's eight pound sledge. The stationmaster stood to one side, helplessly, taut with dismay.

When the men had finished to their satisfaction, they kicked the debris about in contempt, and left the platform. Netfield watched them as they diagonalized northward and entered the Antlers.

He said, "Did that buggy just come in?"

The stationmaster nodded.

"That party was organized," said Netfield. "It wasn't any spur-of-the-moment prank. Who knew that buggy was due?"

"Lots of folks."

"Who was it consigned to?" asked Netfield.

"Andy Efferson," said the stationmaster. "He ordered it from Chicago."

Andy Efferson's only vanity, Netfield knew, was harness-driving.

Harmless Andy, who had never hurt anybody.

"I have a feeling," said the stationmaster thoughtfully, "that Mr. Efferson may have a time getting his money back."

"He'll get his money back," said Netfield curtly. Breathing deeply, he said, "You and I were witnesses."

"I'm not a witness to nothing," said the stationmaster. "I'm not even here. I'm over to the Jerome House, delivering a telegram, I think."

"Well," said Netfield after a moment. "I guess I can't really blame you. Sitting at your desk here by a lamp, on a dark night, you'd make a mighty good target."

About nine that night, he was in his backroom office at the Blue Banner, when there was a conspiratorial knock at the door. He opened it. The Turtle Creek Kid, dusty from travel, stood on the doorstep, blinking and wiping his nose with his thumb. "Well, I'm back," he said importantly. "What next?"

"Why don't you go back home to Mobeeti?" said Netfield kindly. "You have been a wonderful help, and I couldn't have gotten along without you, but why don't you call it a job, and pull out?"

"Why?" asked the Kid suspiciously.

"For one thing, because I like you."

"Oh, no you don't," said the Kid crossly. "Not to me, you don't. You don't make no contract with me and then try to bellycrawl out o' it. And besides—"

"Beside what?" asked Netfield.

"Forget it."

"Besides what?"

"Besides," said the Kid, "I'm a ole man. You're the first customer I had in three year." His voice became suddenly gravelly. "I'm blamed if I'm goin' back to starvin'."

"There are things worse than being hungry," said Netfield softly.

"In the first place," said the Kid, "there's nothing worse than being hungry. And in the second place, this here job's just a big fiesta."

XVI

TINKLING music and drunken argument came from the saloons along Main Street as Netfield made his way up the boardwalk and turned into Efferson's store. Within, the big store lights had been extinguished, and Efferson, standing by a shelf at the rear, was preparing the two small-wick, big-bowled night lights. His face showed strain. At the sight of Netfield, he said, "I suppose you heard of the bacchanal at the station this afternoon?"

"I saw it," said Netfield. "But I had no idea until it was all over that the buggy belonged to you. I thought I'd better come in and feel your pulse, and find out which way you're going to jump."

"I never felt better, thank you," said Efferson calmly. "I know the identities of the parties involved. When I lock up the store, I'm going to search them out . . . separately or together."

"Well, you'll sure as hell find them," said Netfield patiently. "I have a feeling they're waiting around just crying to be found. You don't stand a chance."

"We'll cross that bridge when we come to it."

"We'll cross that bridge right now, right here," said Netfield. "You've got more than your share of guts, Andy. But don't let them trick you into suicide."

"Why not, if the idea appeals to me?"

"You're no warrior, Andy. You're one of the finest humans I ever knew, but you're no warrior. They're coming at me from around the edges, through my friends. Don't let them feed you into the sausage grinder just to upset me."

"You want me to swallow my manhood, is that it?"

"For the time being, yes."

"Would you in a like situation?"

"No, Andy, but you're smarter than I am."

Stony rebellion came into Andy Efferson's tired scholarly eyes.

"Listen," said Netfield. "There was a little point in that buggy-smashing business that maybe you missed. *There were C Bar C men involved.* This shows that Colfax wasn't the only C Bar C man in the Dunphy ring. My guess is that most of Miss Cimarron's men are loyal and honest, but undoubtedly she has hidden outlaws in her bunkhouse. Now you can see the real importance of that buggy smashing."

"To trick me into suicide, you said."

"That, but more than that. You actually mean nothing to them, one way or the other. The real purpose of the thing was to make a public demonstration of an implied brotherhood between 7 Diamond and C Bar C. For a long time they've been trying to keep this very idea secret. Now they want to advertise it. Ranch crews are mighty solid, mighty loyal to each other. In an emergency, they'd all come

out on the same side. A few renegades are trying to commit
the others, and it might well work."

Efferson was appalled.

"But here is the important point, said Netfield. "Dunphy
has put out the word: *Now is the time!*"

When Efferson made no answer, Netfield said casually,
"Kruger has come back to town."

"And after it's all over," said Efferson, "Cimarron will
come in and pick up the pieces."

"Cimarron herself could well be one of the pieces," said
Netfield.

Two days went by, sultry, dreary, listless days for Kirkville, but days of mounting strain for Netfield.

Now was the time, he knew. It could come any minute,
any way.

He walked the streets openly, challengingly, hoping to
tempt the thing to an end—but there was no answer to his
challenge. And as he made his daily rounds, business and
social, stiff-walking and grave, he was sometimes accompanied by Wingate, sometimes by his side, sometimes across
the street and a little to his rear; accompanied by a childlike golden-haired Wingate who seemed incapable of tension
or strain. The Turtle Creek Kid, Netfield noted wryly,
was scarcer than hen's teeth. On occasion, however, Netfield
caught a glimpse of him. Once he saw him, one boot off,
sitting on the edge of the public water-trough, peeling a corn
from his toe with a piece of broken bottle. Once Netfield
almost bumped into him as he came out from the swinging
doors of Ihlmann's pop-skull saloon. On this occasion, he
spoke to Netfield. He said, "Would you like me to lend you
five dollars, Mr. Netfield?"

"No," said Netfield, a little startled.

"Then how about this," said the old man. "How about you
lending *me* five dollars?"

Netfield laughed, and handed him a double eagle.

He was truly getting to love this old man.

Sometimes, too, he saw Cimarron: perhaps coming out of
a shop door from trading, perhaps on her carriage seat as
she stepped her matched blacks down Main Street. On these
occasions, he lifted his hat and spoke, and was answered
with great restraint, almost imperceptibly.

When there was a breeze at all in Kirkville these days,
it came from a distance, from over the baking prairies, as
though from a furnace mouth. The morning-glory vines on
outhouse arbors shriveled and withered. Man and animal
moved in stupor, and the store fronts along Main Street
hung stark and raw in a pall of perpetual dust.

In any Western town, Netfield knew, even under ordinary
circumstances, this season of lethargy could well be a season
of insane and unexpected terror.

Only Cantrell, the new sheriff, seemed not to feel the heat.
Now and then Netfield would pass him on the sidewalk. He
was always spruce in a clean white shirt, as befitting the
importance of his office. They scarcely spoke when they met,
but their eyes communicated their mutual esteem.

Sometimes, too, he saw Dunphy. Dunphy seemed preoc-
cupied, but amiable.

The heat scorched and withered. Dunphy became more
amiable. Efferson became touchy and nervous. Wingate remained placid. Cimarron became pale and withdrawn.

Time crawled.

Thursday morning, about ten o'clock, Netfield was standing
in the entrance way of Efferson's store, chatting with his
friend, when the child suddenly appeared. In this section of
Main Street, the boardwalk was raised about three feet
above road level. Netfield and Efferson were talking, gazing
out over the road, when a child's arm and head popped up
from beneath the boardwalk almost at their feet, and the
child itself scrambled over the edge and stood before them.
It was about eight years old, dirt-smeared, and seemed entirely sexless. It was barefooted and wore a little girl's skirt
stuffed into a little boy's overalls.

Smiling, Netfield said, "Well, hello there. You're Winifred McDonald, aren't you?"

It was Winifred's father who was his swing-man at the Blue Banner.

Mutely, the child nodded.

"How did you get so dirty?" asked Netfield.

"I come down Market Alley to the back door of the Mockingbird, through the Mockingbird, and for the past block I been crawling under the walk. They said at the Mockingbird you were here."

"I am," said Netfield amiably. "What seems to be the trouble?"

"Some fellows have got daddy back in Whitmore's wagon yard."

"Andy," said Netfield softly. "Take Winifred inside and give her the biggest piece of molasses candy you can find."

He started up the walk, and Efferson said, "Don't, George, not alone. It's a trap. Let me get the sheriff."

"I want no sheriffs," said Netfield over his shoulder.

At the first alley mouth, he turned north and broke into a pounding run. He wondered where Wingate was.

Whitmore's wagon yard was a block and a half north of Main Street; it was at the end of a short, blind alley, and was actually an enlargement of the alley-end. It was once a wagon-repair yard, with equipment for putting on rims, shaping tongues and spokes and beds, and mending chains. Whitmore, its owner, however, was taking increasingly to the bottle and now, for long stretches, it lay empty and neglected. It was separated from the alley that fed it by a pair of tall timber gates, and now, as Netfield approached, he found the gates wide open.

Keeping his gun carefully in its holster, he walked through the portals.

He was in a quadrangle perhaps fifty yards square, bordered by low, ramshackle sheds, woodworking and ironworking shops. The large open center was of beaten earth, and here a tableau was waiting for him. All told, he counted seven enemies—and two friends.

His two friends were in a mighty bad way. A little to his left, Wingate lay spread-eagled on the dried horse dung of the ground, his shoulder sodden with blood. Above him, lazily, stood two 7 Diamond men, smirking. When Wingate saw Netfield, he said only, "No."

A dozen feet from Wingate stood the main group, loosely scattered. Netfield's eyes first rested on Dunphy, who was watching Netfield's advance with a fixed, mirthless smile. Dunphy held Wingate's Winchester. The four others of Netfields enemies were also watching him, and of these, three were known to sight to Netfield as 7 Diamond hands. The last he knew instantly must be Kruger, but he passed him with his eyes to look at McDonald.

McDonald stood by an old wagon bed raised on sawhorses. He stood with his back to the others, his arms folded across his face, his forehead leaning against the side of the wagon bed, slumped and boneless, as though he were sleeping on his feet, or soundlessly weeping. Only a patch of the back of his jaw showed, and that was as raw as steak. He had been badly beaten.

When Netfield reached Wingate, he dropped to his heels and asked, "How many did you stop?"

"One," said Wingate through dry lips. "Just above the heart, I think. Goodbye, Mr. Netfield. It's you they're after. You shouldn't have come."

Netfield got to his feet. He passed Dunphy without a glance, wove his way through the 7 Diamond men, passed so close to Kruger that he brushed Kruger's vest, and laid his hand on McDonald's shoulder.

While they watched him stonily, he said, "You're going to be all right, Mac. I don't think they'll bother you anymore. I'm cutting you and Nora in on the Blue Banner, and I'm cutting Sherrod in too. Just tell Efferson I said so."

"Without turning, in a deep voice, as though from a torn

throat, McDonald said, "You shouldn't have come, Mr. Net-field."

Now Dunphy spoke. He said, "Don't be worrying about Mr. Wingate and Mr. McDonald, Mr. Netfield. Nobody's going to bother them anymore. We need them as witnesses— as witnesses that you weren't killed no-show. My friends and I expect to be around Kirkville for a long time, and we want this perfectly legal."

"Was it legal to beat McDonald up?" asked Netfield.

"Yes," said Dunphy. "He abused Kruger with vile language, and Kruger objected."

"Was it legal to wound Sherrod?"

"Yes. He walked up carrying a rifle. We told him to drop it, and when he didn't we shot him."

"We?"

"Kruger."

Netfield turned slowly, and faced Kruger.

This was the first time he had ever set eyes on the man and he studied him carefully. He fitted the picture Netfield had so painstakingly assembled: rawbone, slump-shouldered, big. He was dressed in the shoddiest of ranch-work clothes— as a man who scorned finery—and the Apache moccasins on his huge feet were shapeless and bulging. His nose was flat to his cheekbones, seemingly without bone, and his eyes, milky-blue, seemed the eyes of a blind man, unwavering, lifeless. His single gun had a buckhorn handle; he wore it in a cutdown holster, slightly canted from his thigh.

He was all beast, and would move, Netfield knew, with the unhampered, electric speed of a beast.

"I've been looking for you," said Netfield.

"Well, now you've found me," said Kruger. His voice had an eerie, velvety quality about it.

Deliberately, in a quiet gesture of contempt, Netfield moved his gaze from this man and swept it about the others, as though he had dismissed Kruger and searched further for his true point of danger. The eyeballs of the 7 Diamond men glittered dryly with bloodlust. Even Dunphy, though he tried to conceal his emotions, had an unclean, hungry look about him.

"Are you going to make your move?" asked Kruger. "Or am I going to have to beat you up like I did McDonald?"

"I'm thinking," said Netfield.

"About what?" asked Dunphy.

"About how Sherrod got shot," said Netfield. "It was you, Web, who told him to drop his Winchester but it was Kruger who shot him. The same kind of thing could happen again. It could be you, or any of the others, or all of the others, who would cut loose on me if I moved on Kruger." After a moment, he added, "These animals, all of them, look crazy to count coup."

"If they cut loose, it'll be in self-defense," said Dunphy drolly. "That's a risk you'll have to take. I don't see you have any choice."

In the northwest corner of the yard, beyond McDonald, between a lean-to forge and an open-shed carpenter's bench, was a small door in the log wall. This door slammed open, and a man stumbled in.

He seemed in a wild hurry. He staggered awkwardly, reeled, and caught his balance.

It was the Turtle Creek Kid, and apparently he was being pursued.

Once inside, he flattened himself against the wall and peered warily around the doorsill, in the direction from which he had come. Cautiously, he stretched forth his leg, and, using his boot-toe, closed the door.

He then turned and faced the watching men.

His face squinted in a joyous grin, he ambled across the yard in their direction.

Folded tenderly in the cradle of his left arm, he carried a yellow hound-dog pup, about six months old.

"Now some of you fellers think I stole this dawg," he said with a chuckle. "But I didn't. I jest borrowed him."

XVII

A DOZEN feet away, so that he was the apex of a triangle formed now by the men about Wingate, and the men about Netfield, the Kid came to a clumsy halt and, bending over, placed the dog on the earth. It began immediately to scratch fleas.

Some of the 7 Diamond men smiled arrogantly, some frowned. Dunphy looked momentarily confused. Only Kruger showed no reaction whatever. He was uninterested in dogs or old men; he was interested only in Netfield.

When the Kid straightened, he was arranged for action. His shoulders were slightly hunched, his bandy knees were slightly spread, and his grimy, withered hands were laxly cupped, almost touching his gunbutts.

"All right, Mr. Netfield," he said crossly. "You're safe now. Go home."

Dunphy said, "Who in the hell are you?"

"The sheriff's on his way, Mr. Netfield," said the Kid. "But a lot can happen before then. Better go, while goin's good."

Dunphy broke and reached first. Kruger reached second, but his draw passed Dunphy's—and came to nothing. Netfield was a quarter-turn away from the Kid, watching the two men. The Kid's first two shots slammed out Kruger's life as though he had been sledgehammered. His third shot caught Dunphy, panicked and jerking, in the lower throat, flinging him to the ground, where he died spasmodically trenching the earth with his teeth.

Now Netfield had come into action, wounding one 7 Diamond man and killing another: the two most dangerous, the two by Wingate who were in a position to offer crossfire.

As Netfield spun to engage the others, he got his first good look at the Kid plying his trade. And it was a sight that Netfield never forgot, for it was a sight not only of artistry but of perfect, practiced craftsmanship. Here was one of the cream of the professionals, he knew; one of the truly great ones who had patiently schooled from themselves all error. As deliberately as though he were threading a needle, and yet not so deliberately as to lose that critical instant of advantage, the Kid thumbed back his hammer and slapped it meticulously into his cartridge caps. He fought in true, expert two-gun style; only the gun in his right hand firing; the gun in his left hand held as a tool, in reserve.

The three remaining 7 Diamond men broke wildly and ran.

The Kid holstered his guns, and glanced about him. "Whur's the dawg?" he asked.

In a far corner of the yard, the pup thrust out his scrawny head from behind a rain barrel.

"Gun-shy," explained the Kid affectionately.

Netfield expelled his breath. "So am I, from now on."

Up the alley and through the gate came a small body of townsmen, headed by Sheriff Cantrell and Efferson.

Grimly, Cantrell said, "You've done Kirk County a mighty fine favor, Mr. Netfield."

"Not me," said Netfield. He pointed to the Kid. "Him."

The Kid nodded in agreement. "That's right. Me."

"I'll take over from here," said Cantrell.

"Fine," said Netfield. "Please put Sherrod and McDonald in the best two rooms the Jerome House has to offer. And get the doctor for them. I have business back in town."

To Wingate, he said, "What happened, Sherrod?"

Wingate shifted, grimaced, and said, "I saw Dunphy coming out of the Antlers with this man in moccasins. I locked up the Banner, and followed them. They went down a couple of alleys and ended up here in the wagon yard. Those 7 Diamond men were waiting for them with McDonald. I was afraid for McDonald, so they got me."

"Well, take it easy," said Netfield. "What can I do for you?"

"Bring over that other gentleman," said Wingate.

"What gentleman?" said Netfield.

"The gentleman with you. The gentleman that did all the shooting."

Netfield gestured, and the Kid joined them.

Wingate and the Kid stared at each other.

"I never knowed you was a gunfighter," said Wingate.

"You never knowed a lot of things," said the Kid. "You ain't out of yore diapers yet."

Wingate's eyes glowed happily. "Mr. Netfield, this-here's the snottiest talker I met since I crossed the Mississippi."

"Naturally," said the Kid.

"You're one of the meanest, dirtiest, nastiest humans I ever laid eyes on," said Wingate respectfully.

"O' course," said the Kid. "And that's because I keep my wits about me."

To Netfield, Wingate said, "He puts me in mind of my daddy back in Tennessee."

"If I had sired you," said the Kid, "I'd have gone behind the biggest manure pile I could find, and blowed out my brains."

"Yes, sir," said Wingate joyously.

As Netfield and the Kid walked back to Main Street, the Kid said, "You know, that Wingate feller is one of the nicest meanest mortals I ever run into."

"Yes, indeed," said Netfield. "And I should say that describes him perfectly."

At the corner of Main and Maple, as they were about to separate, Netfield said, "You saved my life back there. I can't say anything more. Just that."

"What's your life, what's mine, what's Dunphy's?" asked the Kid. "Nothing." His grimy face looked waxen and withdrawn. "Ain't this a hell of a way for a ole man like me to earn his bread and butter? You know something? For forty-one years I been downright ashamed o' myself."

Before the day was out, and increasingly in the days that

followed, Netfield found himself the town hero. With the wagon yard fight, 7 Diamond was broken, and the plan to use the Kirkville Feeding Yards as an outlet for stolen cattle collapsed. Cantrell spread the true story, and Efferson, and Cimarron.

Most remarkable of all the events occurring in this interval was, in Netfield's opinion, Cimarron's new attitude. She publicly reversed herself, and this he well knew, took great honesty and courage. In every way possible, she showed her respect and gratitude for Netfield.

As the excitement died down, an uneasiness came upon him, an uneasiness that grew. He wondered if he were in love with her. If he had been in love with her all along, but just too damned busy to realize it?

One sticky night he put on his best frock coat and called on her in the parlor of her home to discuss it with her. She was waiting for him, dressed in crisp ice-blue tafteta, and received him timidly but warmly. He began by discussing other things.

"More than anything," he said, "Sherrod Wingate wants desperately to return to his homestead, to the farm he cleared and built up. Dunphy took it by fraud. Now Dunphy is gone. I'm going to try to get it returned to Sherrod, legally and quickly."

"I think we'll have no trouble there," she said. "I have a little influence, and I'll use it to hurry things along."

Netfield nodded.

"Can I ask you a favor?" said Netfield.

"Any favor in the world."

"This is about Cantrell," said Netfield. "He's an ex-cowman, and I'll bet a blasted good one. I don't think he's too happy in his present work. C Bar C needs a full-time foreman, now that Elton Colfax has pulled out. Give Cantrell a try. You'll help him, and you'll help yourself."

"Of course," she said. "And I thank you for your advice."

After a moment, she said, "Anything else?"

"Well, yes," he said.

"What?"

"I think I'm in love with you. Could that be?"

Her eyes seemed glazed with diamonds.

When she spoke, she said, "It better be. Or your real trouble, George Netfield, is just starting."

Later, as he left her on the doorstep, she said, "The Antlers is a rat nest, George. I'm going to sell it."

"No," he said. "That would be a coward's way. The next owner would simply inherit, and probably increase, its wickedness. Keep it, and clean it up."

"Will you take over the responsibility? Will you clean it up for me?"

"Yes," he said, grinning wolfishly. "I will indeed."

XVIII

THE FOLLOWING week a collection of the county's most influential citizens, shopkeepers, ranchers, professional men, assembled in Andy Efferson's store room to discuss the choice of a new sheriff. Netfield was present, not only by right but by special invitation, and he soon saw that he was the number one nominee. He declined persistently and, finally, forcefully.

"Then who will we get?" asked a rancher from the northern part of the county.

"Just any man won't do," said the owner of the Mockingbird. "Give in to us, George."

"No," said Netfield.

Efferson said, "We all realize now Kirk County had a close call. We can't run that risk again. We need a sheriff that's a topnotch man."

"Agreed," said Netfield. "Why don't you ask Miss Ernestine to find one for you?"

"Miss Ernestine?" said a rancher. "You mean the old woman that keeps the parlor-house?"

Netfield nodded.

A rumble of distaste and dissension ran through the gathering.

The rancher said, "Are you serious, Mr. Netfield?"

Netfield didn't bother to answer.

Hesitantly, Efferson said, "We'll try it if you advise it, George."

"You won't regret it," said Netfield. He picked up his hat to leave. "Meet her as an equal, talk to her as an equal, and tell her your problem. She'll get you a sheriff."

At the doorway, he turned. "He might come from Kansas, or Oregon, or Arkansas, but, by God, when he gets off the train you'll be looking at a real man."

That day, too, Wingate and the Kid left Kirkville to move into Wingate's abandoned homestead. They left subsidized by a committee of grateful citizens, headed by Cimarron, with two wagons, a team of mules in lead, a new plowpoint, chickens, two cows, staples, and a next-year's order for seed. Since the fray in the wagon yard, Wingate and the Kid had merged in a close companionship, in a weird sort of father-and-son relationship. They had become inseparable. It was as though they had found in each other families that they had long ago lost. Netfield marveled to watch them together; the Kid stern and opinionated and unreasonable, Wingate meek and mannerly and always polite with a yes-sir or no-sir.

As they moved their miniature wagon train south, down Main Street, diminishing in a blossom of dust, Cimarron and Netfield waved them goodbye.

"Well, there they go," said Cimarron. "And that's something I'd like to see sometime with my own eyes, the Turtle Creek Kid pushing a plow."

"Don't let that old man fool you," said Netfield. "I'll bet if he decides to farm, he'll really farm."

"They'll be C Bar C neighbors, on the south," said Cimarron. "I'm glad."

"The whole county should be glad," said Netfield. "We've got a good brace of watchdogs down near the passmouth now. There's a pair that will really keep an eye south, towards Bonnet County."